OPAL

A WOLFES OF MANHATTAN NOVEL

HELEN HARDT

HARDT & SONS

OPAL

A WOLFES OF MANHATTAN NOVEL

Helen Hardt

WWW.HELENHARDT.COM

For my amazing beta readers—Karen Aguilera, Serena Drummond, Linda Pantlin Dunn, and Angela Tyler.

You ladies rock!

PRAISE FOR HELEN HARDT

"Christian, Gideon, and now...Braden Black."
~**Books, Wine, and Besties** on *Follow Me Darkly*

"This red-hot tale will have readers fanning themselves."
~**Publishers Weekly** on *Blush*

"Scintillating..."
~**Publishers Weekly** on *Bloom*

"An absolute must-read. With its engaging plot and enthralling characters, this novel keeps you hooked from start to finish."
~**The Llama Library** on *Bloom*

"Helen's intelligent writing style and skills have made this story a must-read."
~**FireSerene Reads** on *Bloom*

"It's hot, it's intense, and the plot starts off thick and had me completely spellbound from page one."
~**The Sassy Nerd Blog** on *Rebel*

"This book was fantastic! It was steamy, funny, romantic, and just about any other emotion you can think of..."
~**Steamy Book Mama** on *Lily and the Duke*

"The writing was fast paced and *hot* for a historical romance...with lots of chemistry...and a lot of fun!
~**Bound by Books** on *Lily and the Duke*

"*Craving* is the jaw-dropping book you *need* to read!"
~*New York Times* **bestselling author Lisa Renee Jones** on

WOLFES OF MANHATTAN READING ORDER

Rebel
Recluse
Runaway
Rake
Reckoning
Escape
Moonstone
Raven
Garnet
Buck
Opal
Phoenix
Amethyst

WARNING

This book contains adult language and scenes, including flashbacks of physical and sexual abuse. Please take note.

PROLOGUE
ASPEN

Buck and I get married at Luke and Katelyn's beach house.

I was surprised Buck agreed to it, but he and Luke seem to have finally come to an understanding between them.

Katelyn and I are ecstatic about it. Because we're besties, the four of us will be spending a lot of time together.

Katelyn is, of course, my maid of honor, and Buck's sister Emily is my bridesmaid. Coming back to this house couldn't have been easy for her, but she did it for Buck and for me.

Buck has two best men. His brother, Johnny, and his fellow SEAL, Leif Ramsey. Also known as Phoenix.

I'm dancing with Phoenix later. He's tall and muscular, like Buck, but there the similarities end. Leif is blond and blue-eyed with light skin.

"Thank you for being here," I tell him. "For Buck. It means everything to him."

"I'll always be here for Buck," Leif says. "We're brothers."

His phone buzzes.

"Do you mind?"

"Of course not."

He leads me off the dance floor and looks at his phone.

"Oh, shit."

"Is anything the matter?"

"I need to talk to Buck."

"Leif, this is our wedding day. Please..."

"I know, Aspen. And I'm sorry."

Buck is on the dance floor with his sister.

Emily and Luke seem to have made their peace as well, and for that I'm grateful. Emily is radiant—she looks like Buck in female form—and she seems ecstatic with her significant other, Scotty, a half-Hawaiian surfer boy who's now studying to be a licensed psychologist.

A moment later, Buck is leaving the dance floor with Leif. They go inside the house.

I wait.

And I wait.

Only a few minutes have passed, but I can't take it any longer. I head into the house to find them.

They're deep in conversation when—

"Aspen, baby."

"Exactly what's going on?"

"I'm so sorry," Buck says, "but I need to go back to New York."

"All right. In two weeks. After our trip to the Virgin Islands."

"I promise you, baby, we will have the honeymoon of the century. But we have to put it off for a little while."

The spoiled little girl inside me wants to stomp and hold my breath, but I don't. This is Buck. The man who loves me.

And he wouldn't make me postpone my honeymoon unless it was very important.

He is who he is. He's Buck. He saves people. He wouldn't be the man I love if he didn't do that.

"Why? What is it?"

"It's another one of the women from the island." Buck shakes his head. "Opal. She's in trouble."

I swallow. "Kelly?"

Kelly was different. She used to get jealous when someone was chosen over her. None of us understood her. Of course, none of us tried to understand anything while we were there. We were simply trying to keep our own heads above water.

"Yeah," Phoenix says. "A threat has been made against her...by another woman from the island."

1

LEIF

Cheating Buck and Aspen out of their honeymoon wasn't on my to-do list, but the Wolfe family pays us big money to take care of these women and keep them safe.

They even sent their private jet to bring us back from LA to New York. Aspen insisted on coming with us, and even though Buck and I both tried to talk her out of it, that woman has a mind of her own.

Buck is worried for her safety, and so am I, but from what I can tell, the woman can take care of herself. She's tall, strong, athletic. Gorgeous with dark hair and eyes. She and Buck will make beautiful kids.

Damn.

Kids.

I can't believe Buck is married. That last tour of duty fucked both of us up so bad, I wasn't sure either of us would be able to have a decent relationship, but Buck defied the odds. He and Aspen are perfect together.

As for me? I'm not looking. I don't think I'll ever look.

Definitely too fucked up. Torture and violation... We're prepared for it during training, but can you ever be truly prepared?

No.

You can't.

Buck and I are meeting Reid and Rock Wolfe at their office this morning, and of course Aspen is tagging along. Once we get through security in the Wolfe building, we take the elevator to the main office and check in with the receptionist.

"The Wolfes are expecting you," the receptionist says with a smile. "Have a seat, and someone will come get you soon."

I plunk my ass down on a comfortable couch in the reception area. Buck and Aspen sit across from me on another couch, Aspen twiddling her thumbs.

Buck and I both rise when Reid Wolfe, dressed in his signature navy-blue tailored suit, walks out to greet us. Fatherhood suits him. He looks more at ease these days. When I first met Reid, he was a stiff businessman who had no time for anything but work—unless it was a quick fuck with his woman du jour. Now he's a devoted family man, married to one of his father's victims and a father himself to an adorable infant girl.

"Buck, Leif." Reid shakes our hands, and then his gaze falls on Aspen. "Ms. Davis, I'm glad you came along. You may be able to offer some insight."

Aspen shakes Reid's hand. "It's Mrs. Moreno now." She smiles. "But Aspen is fine. And that's why I'm here. I want to help."

"I know we're asking a lot of you and your new husband, postponing your honeymoon for a little while, but we think this might be serious." He nods to the receptionist. "I don't want to be disturbed during this meeting. Not at all."

"Yes, Mr. Wolfe."

Then to us, "Follow me."

Buck, Aspen, and I follow Reid through the winding hallways to one of the conference rooms. I've been in this particular room many times, but it always leaves me in awe. It's huge, of course, with a solid cherry table that seats up to twenty. The chairs are cushioned with blue and gold brocade, but the most iconic part of the room are its walls. They're home to a triptych of paintings by Roy Wolfe, and whenever I look at them—abstract in blues, golds, grays, and whites—I see something different. Today I see the ocean...but perhaps that's because I was just in LA at a house on the beach for Buck's wedding.

When we enter, Rock—Reid's oldest brother and chief executive officer of Wolfe Enterprises—stands.

He looks a little rougher than Reid, who always looks refined. But there's no mistaking the resemblance between them. Only their eyes are different—Reid's are blue and Rock's are green. But they both have the same determination in their gazes.

"You all know my brother Rock."

Rock shakes hands all around. "Good to see you. Thank you for coming. My wife, Lacey, will be here in a minute." He gazes at the doorway. "Here she is now."

Lacey Wolfe is blond and blue-eyed, and she's just starting to show a baby bump.

"Mrs. Wolfe," I say, "nice to see you again. And congratulations."

"Thank you, Leif. And please call me Lacey."

"You know my friend, Buck Moreno, and this is his wife, Aspen."

A smile spreads across Aspen's face when I say the word "wife."

Lacey shakes both their hands and holds onto Aspen's a bit longer. "I just want to tell you that you're amazing. And thank you for coming. We all feel so terrible about ruining your honeymoon."

Aspen attempts a smile. "Buck and I will have a honeymoon. I just feel so fortunate that, after all I've been through, I found such an amazing life for myself. So I want to help Kelly."

"All of you ladies are amazing," Lacey says. "Your strength and fortitude humble me."

"That's kind of you," Aspen says, "but your family made sure we got the best mental health treatment on the island."

"Yes, Riley and Matt have done an incredible job with the treatment center. I'm so glad it was helpful to you and the others."

"Most of the others anyway," Reid says. "Please, have a seat. All of you."

"So what's the story?" I ask. "Which woman has been making threats against Kelly?"

2

KELLY

I won't rest until I see you back on that island.

I shiver as I read the latest text message.

Haven't I been through enough? I'm finally learning to accept my life, my past, work through not only my time on the island but my childhood as well. The therapist hired by the Wolfe family, Macy, has been great. I have to commend the patience she has with me.

I'm not an easy person to deal with.

I never knew that until recently, but now I'm beginning to see why I do some of the things I do.

Why I was the way I was on the island.

Why I am the way I am now, and how to go about making the changes that I want—need—to make in my life.

But someone *doesn't* want that.

And I don't understand why, because she has the same past that I have.

Her name is Brindley.

Brindley McGregor. But her name on the island was Smoky. Short for smoky quartz, because of her grayish eyes.

Her eyes aren't gray so much as bluish gray, but she was one of the last women to come to the island before it was shut down, and maybe they were running out of gemstone names.

I was known as Opal, and honestly I'm not sure why. My hair is auburn and my eyes are dark blue. Opal seems more of a light-blue name, but who knows? I never stopped to think about why they named me Opal. I didn't care.

I just accepted my fate. I accepted it because I figured it was all I deserved.

After all, my childhood was…

Less than adequate.

I laugh out loud at my own thought.

Less than adequate? What a fucking euphemism. As a rule, I hate euphemisms. Why not be blunt? Why not be offensive? Life is blunt and offensive sometimes. More often than not, in my opinion.

My childhood sucked. I was beaten, locked in closets, told what a piece of shit I was on the daily. Rarely did I get enough to eat.

Life on the island? It sucked too, but at least I was fed. They kept us fed well, because we needed to be strong.

We needed to be worthy prey.

That's what those men paid for.

They wanted to hunt us, like animals. It was a game to them. Once they caught us, they could feel like big strong masculine guys because they had captured worthy prey.

Most of the women there didn't understand me. Hell, why should they? They all came from great backgrounds, decent childhoods. Maybe not perfect childhoods, but were they beaten? Starved for days on end? Locked in closets? Forced to—

I shake my head, refusing to let the words dig into my mind.

I'm trying to work through this stuff, deal with it, but there are still things I can't think about.

I live in the subsidized housing that the Wolfe family put together for us, and I listen, during group therapy, to the other women talk. Lily is here—Tiger Eye from the island— and Katelyn and Aspen have already left. But some new women have arrived—Francine known as Peridot, Marianne known as Pearl, and of course, Brindley.

Smoky herself.

I look at the words on the text again.

I don't know Smoky's background. She only arrived at the building a week ago, but she started texting me right away.

Right when I was breaking through, making progress.

Feeling that maybe I *didn't* deserve to be taken to that island.

Maybe I *didn't* deserve the horrible abuse I suffered as a child.

Maybe I'm better than all of that.

Then here comes Brindley, telling me I'm not.

I stuff my phone into my small purse and leave my apartment. I'm going over to the office building to talk to Reid and Rock Wolfe.

I want to put an end to this once and for all.

3

LEIF

The door to the conference room crashes open.

"Ma'am, please!"

A young woman with reddish-brown hair pulled back in a high ponytail crashes into the room. She's wearing baggy jeans cinched at the waist with a leather belt and a tight T-shirt that shows a sliver of her belly.

Rock rises to his feet. "Danielle, what the hell is going on?"

"I'm sorry, Mr. Wolfe. I tried to stop her. I've alerted security."

Reid rises, shakes his head. "It's all right. Buck, Leif, Aspen, this is Kelly Taylor."

A look of recognition crosses Aspen's fine features. "Hi, Kelly."

Kelly clears her throat. "Garnet. Sorry, I mean Aspen. I hear congratulations are in order."

"Thank you."

The two women are speaking in a weird robotic tone. I get the feeling they don't like each other. Not at all.

That doesn't make a lot of sense to me, given they were in the same boat on the island.

"Ms. Taylor," Rock says. "What can we do for you?"

Kelly pulls the phone out of her purse and shoves it in Rock's face. "I got another one. From Brindley."

"Brindley?" Aspen asks.

"Smoky from the island. Smoky Quartz." Kelly's voice is tinny.

"Right." Aspen nods. "She wasn't there for very long, was she?"

"About six months before we were rescued," Kelly says.

Rock takes the phone from Kelly and studies it. "And you're sure these texts are coming from her?"

"She all but admitted as much."

"This isn't the phone number we have registered for her."

Kelly grabs the phone out of Rock's hand and glares at the screen. "So? She bought her own phone."

"This is a new number," Rock says. "We'll trace it, but I'm pretty sure we'll find the same thing. That it's untraceable. From a burner."

"Where would she be getting burners?" Aspen asks.

"Anywhere," I say. "The question is, where is she getting the money for the burners?"

"We give the ladies a pretty nice allowance," Reid says. "It's the least we can do."

"Who are these guys?" Kelly glares at Buck and me.

But man, even with the glare? She's got to be one of the most beautiful women I've ever laid eyes on. I've always been a sucker for a redhead, and her hair is a nice auburn, just red enough to make my dick react.

Plus, she's got a tight-ass body. Just that little sliver of belly shows me how tight and muscled she is.

13

I love women who are in shape. I met a lot of them in the Armed Forces, and that's what I go for. Same for Buck, which is clearly why he went for Aspen.

I can't help but think about *why* Kelly and Aspen are in shape, though. They were... Ugh. I still can't go there.

And damn, they are beautiful.

Especially Kelly Taylor.

A spitfire too. A personality that goes with that red hair.

I'm not Buck, though. I'm not going to fall for a woman with so much baggage. I don't even like to think about what they went through on that island because then I have to think about what Buck and I have been through. How he and I were the only ones who came home from that last tour. He and I voluntarily joined the Navy, though.

Kelly? Aspen? They were forced to do the unthinkable.

"Buck Moreno and Leif Ramsey," Reid replies to Kelly. "Sorry, I should have made that clear when I introduced them to you. They're part of our security team, and they're here to help us investigate these threats that are being made against you."

"You brought in the brawn to investigate?" Kelly scoffs. "Just bring Brindley in here, force her to tell you she's doing this and then ask her why."

"We don't have any proof that it's Brindley," Rock says.

"You have *me!* I've told you it's her. She admitted it!"

I rise then, reach my hand out to Kelly. "It's good to meet you."

She takes my hand and shakes it hard. "Yeah. So what are you going to do about this?"

Damn.

This one's got a mean streak for sure. I bet she's a fucking tigress in the sack.

Why am I even thinking about that? I *don't* want a woman with all this baggage. Plus, she's rude. Mean. Nasty.

"We're here to get to the bottom of it. Buck and I—along with Aspen—will figure it out."

"Do you feel like your life is in danger?" Buck asks.

"I don't know. The building we're in has security up the yin-yang. But sometimes..."

"Sometimes what?" I prompt.

"She's in the same building I am, as you know. Brindley. Sometimes in the middle of the night, I hear noises. When I get up, I can distinctly hear someone fidgeting with my door-knob. Who else could it be? No one else has access to the building except the people who live here and security."

"We have top-notch security," Reid says. "All the guys are vetted and then vetted again."

"So it's got to be one of the women," Kelly says. "It's not Lily. She's afraid of her own shadow. And Francine and Mari-anne keep to themselves. It has to be Brindley."

"How did she admit to you that she was sending the text?" I ask.

"I got in her face. I accused her. And she didn't deny it."

Buck suppresses a chuckle. "That's hardly an admission, Ms. Taylor."

"You don't know the bitch."

Aspen rises then. "I know her. I remember her just like I remember you. What I recall is—"

"Did I ask you what you recall?" Kelly advances toward Aspen. "I know you hated me on that island. I know you *all* hated me."

"I didn't hate you, Kelly." Aspen smiles with her lips, but it doesn't reach her eyes. It's a look of pity. "I didn't hate anyone. I was trying to survive just like you were."

"You were all jealous of me."

"That's not how I remember it."

"Just how *do* you remember it then?" Kelly demands, her arms across her chest.

Aspen pauses a moment, and I can almost feel her counting to ten. She clearly doesn't want to engage with Kelly but she's getting pissed. Who can blame her?

"I've already told Buck and Leif," Aspen finally says. "How *you* were the jealous one. You didn't like it when someone got chosen over you."

Kelly scoffs. "In what universe does that make any sense?"

"Believe me," Aspen says. "That's what *we* all thought."

Kelly narrows her eyes, and her facial muscles tense further. "Go to hell, Garnet."

Aspen's eyes widen, but she doesn't respond. It's clear she considers reference to their island names a hit below the belt. I admire her ability to ignore Kelly's obvious desire to pick a fight.

"Wait just a minute," Rock says. "My brother and I are very sorry for what you went through on that island, Ms. Taylor. We would erase it from all of you if we could. And we're doing our damnedest to make sure you all get the treatment you need and deserve. But speaking that way to another survivor—to anyone, really—isn't the way to go about that. If you want to be a part of this meeting, then sit down. You're the victim here, so your input is necessary. But leave the attitude outside."

Kelly draws in a breath, and for a moment, I think she's going to shout Rock down.

But Rock Wolfe is nothing if not an imposing presence. He still has the air of a rebel about him.

Kelly draws in a breath. "All right." She heads to an empty seat and sits her ass down.

Her very *nice* ass.

"All right," Reid says. "Let's continue with the meeting."

4

KELLY

I've regressed.

It's clear as day.

I was getting somewhere with therapy. But now? I'm back to accusing people. Treating people badly. Blaming everyone else for the circumstances of my life.

It's funny. I see it unfolding right before me, like a movie on the screen at the cinema.

Regression.

Back to the old Kelly.

Back to Opal.

But I don't want to be Opal anymore.

And I don't want to be Kelly either.

Kelly had to learn to fend for herself, to scrape moldy food from the bottoms of containers she found in the trash to ease the ache of hunger.

I know I shouldn't be acting this way. The whole island situation was Derek Wolfe's doing, not his children's. These people are here to help me. Even Aspen is here to help me.

Why do I act this way?

I need to see Macy.

But before then, I need to sit through this meeting and see what they can do for me.

So I listen—but only with one ear.

Because images emerge in my brain, and though I try to wipe them away, I'm not that strong yet.

The closet is dark.

I don't know how long I've been in here, and my tummy is growling for food. I'm thirsty too, and my mouth is dry. My throat is hurting from the screaming and the crying.

I was a bad girl. And what do bad girls get? They get locked in the dark closet, after they get spanked.

My butt hurts from the spanking, but not like it used to. I'm older now. I just turned ten, and Mama even got me a birthday cake.

She put ten candles on it, lit them, and sang happy birthday to me.

Before she knocked me on the back of my head, pulled me into her lap, spanked me, and then shoved me into the closet.

I sigh in relief when the door opens, and I shield my eyes against the light.

"Come on out now, sweetheart." Mama's voice is soft and kind.

This is my mama. Sweet as syrup in one minute, violent and destructive the next.

She never leaves any marks on me that can be seen. Only where my clothes cover them. Or on the top of the head where they're camouflaged by my orange hair.

The orange hair I hate.

The orange hair that the kids make fun of.

"Come here, sweetheart."

I run into her arms, just like I always do.

Because I love my mama. And I know my mama loves me. She tells me so every day. Between beatings and locking me in the closet.

"I'm so sorry, sweetheart. But you know you have to be a good girl. You know Mama has to punish you when you're bad."

I nod and choke out a sob against her breast. I know better than to ask what I did. That will only set her off again.

But I don't know what I did. I never know what I do.

The closet she locks me in is in the spare room. Not my own closet, where at least I'd have the comfort of my clothes. Just an empty space with wood floor and walls.

I follow her out to the kitchen, where a lone gift sits on the table, wrapped in plain red paper. When I look closer, I see that it's not plain. There's a slightly darker red snowflake pattern on it. It's Christmas wrap. But it was nice of Mama to go to the effort. We don't have a lot of money, so I'm lucky I'm getting a present at all.

I don't dare touch it, though. I've learned to never make assumptions where Mama is concerned.

"Well..." she says. "Go ahead."

I move toward the gift, but I still don't touch it.

"Open your present, Kelly. It's your birthday, after all."

I grab the present off the table and rip it open. It's a cardboard shoebox. New shoes, maybe? I remove the lid.

I gasp out loud.

Inside the shoebox is my volleyball. It's been deflated.

Mama smiles. "Do you like it?"

"I don't understand," I say. "Why did you take all the air out of my volleyball?"

"I didn't just let the air out," Mama says. "I poked holes in it so you can't use it anymore."

Tears well in my eyes.

"You've been spending too much time playing volleyball after school," Mama continues. "I need you home. Things don't get done around here if you're not here to do them."

I gulp back the tears. I stopped crying over Mama's cruelty long ago, but this is beyond callous, even for her.

"But I love playing with the other girls after school."

Mama's face twists into a snarl. "Kelly, I went to all the trouble to get you a gift that will help you to be a better person. A better daughter. You might show a bit more appreciation."

Appreciation? Sadness sweeps through me. I can't cry. I won't cry.

Perhaps she's right. Maybe I'm being selfish. I suppose I don't need my own ball. All the other girls have their own, and we only need one ball to play.

But I saved up money, collected box tops.

And I went around to all the neighbors, asking if they needed any chores done. I made a few bucks that way.

I gulp again. If I start crying, it may set her off.

And I'll end up back in the closet.

So I simply set the box down on the table and look up at my mother. "Thank you for the present, Mama. It was very thoughtful of you."

"You're very welcome, sweetheart. Happy birthday."

5

LEIF

Buck and Aspen are staying in a suite at a posh hotel. Me?

I'm moving into one of the furnished apartments in the building that houses Derek Wolfe's victims.

Why? I don't know. It's not like they need additional security. But after the meeting, Reid took me aside and asked me to do it.

"I want someone watching after Kelly in particular," he says. "I'm not exactly sure what's going on with her. Whether Brindley McGregor is threatening her or not. I need you to talk to Brindley, have her answer some questions."

I furrow my brow. "You mean no one has talked to her?"

"Just a police officer Kelly called after she got the first text. She called the cops before she called any of us."

"And?"

"It went as you would expect. Brindley denied any wrong-doing. She even let us look at her cell phone. But as you know, she could be using burners."

"Kelly is..." I shake my head. "Something's not right there."

"We're not privy to any of her records from the treatment center on Wolfe Island," Reid says. "Doctor-patient confidentiality and all. But her doctors did say she was ready to leave the retreat center and come home."

"Where is home for her?"

"Phoenix, Arizona."

I raise my eyebrows at the word *Phoenix*. It's my Navy SEAL name. But I'm not from Arizona. I'm from Texas. They gave me the name because I was so good at getting out of scrapes—like a phoenix rising from the ashes.

I *am* pretty good at that. That last scrape, though? Only Buck and I got out alive.

"So the cops didn't do anything?"

"What could they do?" Reid shrugs. "Her phone was clean, and Brindley hasn't gone anywhere. She's still getting acclimated. Security footage shows she rarely leaves the building."

"Aspen says Kelly was different on the island," I tell Reid. "She said she would actually get jealous when one of the other girls was picked over her." I shake my head. "I can't imagine why. Aspen and Katelyn both say they considered it a reprieve when they weren't chosen."

Reid closes his eyes for a second. "I can't imagine what those ladies went through. And Zee... It was almost her too."

"The only one that got away."

"I thank God every day." Reid rubs a hand over his face. "I can't even imagine what Buck is going through with Aspen."

"Aspen's in a good place, I think. So is Buck. They're good for each other. It's like they complete each other, and I don't mean that in a ridiculous romantic way. I mean it in a truly symbiotic way. They're like yin and yang."

"They do seem to be well matched," Reid agrees. "I'm happy for them. You know how much you guys mean to me. You've helped me out for the last couple years, helped me solve this mystery to begin with."

"You seem to be in a good place now."

Reid smiles. "I am. With Zee and little Nora. But still, it wasn't that long ago when we were searching those caves under the church. It's crazy what was going on, and my siblings and I had no idea."

"Not even Riley?"

"Riley had her own problems with our father. I think she was probably on that island, but it sounds like he kept her drugged up. And of course, she was his little princess. He never would've put her out on the hunt." Reid grimaces. "God, I can't even think about it."

"It's tough for sure. But don't you worry about Kelly. I'll keep my eye on her."

"She's a handful, I'm afraid."

"She's nice to look at, at least."

"All those women are beautiful. My father wouldn't have had it any other way."

"Buck was telling me how both Katelyn and Aspen got taken. Aspen was screwed over by members of her own volleyball team, and Katelyn by her cousin. God knows what these people were paid to provide beautiful women for abduction and transport to that island."

"I know. Katelyn's cousin is rotting in jail, and everyone behind Aspen's abduction is either dead or in prison. I wish I could say the same about all the men who were on that island. Some of them disappeared into thin air."

"Having billions at your disposal gives you opportunities most of us don't have." I widen my eyes, realizing my implication. "I didn't mean anything by that."

"I know that. Most of us billionaires aren't assholes. We don't use women. We don't traffic women. We run our businesses ethically and legally. My old man?" Reid shakes his head. "I have no idea what was going on in his head, and I don't even want to know. I hope *this* apple falls very far from that tree."

"And all the others. What you've done on that island in such a short time is amazing."

"The retreat center and the art colony are doing well, and the resort will open soon. I hope you'll join us down there for the grand opening."

"That's probably above my pay grade, buddy."

"Are you kidding? After all you and Buck have done for our family? You'll be our guests, all first-class accommodations, gratis."

"I may take you up on that. In the meantime, I'll make sure Kelly Taylor's taken care of."

"You're a good man, Leif. Or should I call you Phoenix?"

"Leif is good. Buck goes by his SEAL name because it was always his nickname anyway. The rest of us go by our regular names."

Flashback then...to my dead buddies. My heart races. Why did I use the present tense?

"The rest of us went by our regular names," I clarify. "Buck and I are the only two left."

Reid says nothing. What can he say?

We head into the building and stop at the security desk.

"Mr. Wolfe," the guard on duty says.

"Good afternoon, Royal. This is Leif Ramsey, and he's

going to be taking apartment 405. He's on my personal payroll, security duty. He'll be watching specifically over Kelly Taylor."

"Excuse me?" An angry female voice says. "He will be *what*?"

6

KELLY

"Ms. Taylor," the man named Leif says.

"I don't need a freaking babysitter."

"He's not a babysitter, Kelly," Reid says. "He's security for you. Plain and simple. There have been threats made against you, and we're still not sure where—"

"I've told you. It's Brindley."

"She denies it, and we don't have proof. But someone is making those threats, and I want to make sure you are adequately protected." Reid rakes his fingers through his short black hair. "Leif here is the best. He's an ex-Navy SEAL, and he's been working for me for years. He has my complete faith and confidence."

"Isn't it more important that he have *my* complete faith and confidence?" I regard Leif Ramsey. He's tall and broad and gorgeous, of course. Blond hair and blue eyes, fair skin. An obvious Nordic type. "Are you some kind of Viking?"

"My mother is of Norwegian descent," he says. "My father's family comes from the UK. I assure you my ethnicity has nothing to do with my qualifications."

"I don't care about your qualifications," I say. "Consider yourself fired."

"Fine by me." Leif shoves his hands into the pockets of his jeans.

"He's not on your payroll, Ms. Taylor," Reid says. "He's on mine. I own this building, and Mr. Ramsey will be occupying apartment 405."

"Isn't that cozy? Since I'm in 407."

"All of you ladies are on the fourth floor, may I remind you," Reid says.

"Yeah, but you put this clown right next to me."

Leif shakes his head. "Dude, you're not paying me *enough*."

"You're absolutely right," Reid says. "Let me triple what I'm paying you for this job."

"Why don't you quadruple it," I say, "because I sure am *not* going to make it easy for him."

"Good enough." Reid nods. "Quadruple it is, Leif. Enjoy yourself. Come on. Let me show you to your place."

I follow them since I'm going up anyway. Inside the elevator, I feel cramped between these two broad-shouldered men.

Some of the women on the island were very tall—Aspen, for example. She was a professional volleyball player. Which meant every time I looked at her, I remembered my mother crushing my volleyball dreams all those years ago.

But that wasn't Aspen's fault. The year of therapy on the island convinced me of that.

I was fucked up.

I'm still fucked up, but I'm learning.

And regressing...

I haven't made it easy for the Wolfe family, even though I know none of this was their fault. It took me a while to accept that. I mean, how could their father have been doing all of this without anyone finding out about it?

Especially Reid, who worked side-by-side with his father at his company? The other three weren't involved in his business, so it's a little easier to give them a pass. But Reid? The guy in the elevator with me right now?

I'm having a hard time forgiving him.

Plus, he's married to the one woman who managed to get away. Her name is Zinnia, Zee for short. Somehow, she escaped before she got to the island. I don't know the whole story, although she's made it clear that she's willing to talk to any of us if we'd like to.

Maybe one day I will. She has a new baby at home, though.

How could she fall in love with Reid Wolfe? The son of the man who kidnapped her, nearly sent her to that horrific place?

The elevator dings as we reach the fourth floor. When the doors open, Reid and the Navy SEAL guy both stand there.

Gentlemen? I guess they're waiting for me to go out. Ladies first and all.

I suppose I should be flattered, but instead I'm more pissed off.

Seems I'm always pissed off.

Macy says I'm making amazing progress, but the other women here don't seem nearly as angry as I am.

"We all go at our own speed," Macy said to me once, "and your doctors at the retreat center wouldn't have sent you back here if they didn't feel you were ready."

Of course, I've always wondered if they sent me here because they were tired of dealing with me. I didn't make it easy for them, either. I walked out on several sessions, and that was tame compared to the time I hurled a book at a timid therapist named Dr. Nook. I never saw her again. Instead, I got a male therapist, Dr. Sweeney. I didn't hurl a book at him. I hurled a paperweight from his desk, and I just missed his temple.

After that, I had a chaperone for sessions until they could trust me again.

I've never made it easy for anyone in my life, and it's not that I don't want to. I don't want to feel like this. It's horrible, feeling agitation and resentment all the time.

The only time I feel relaxed is when I'm in a session with Macy, and then for a couple hours afterward. Talking to her helps me, but then I go back to my old ways.

I walk to my apartment, and Reid and the blond guy head to the one next door.

Reid slides his key card through the reader, and the door clicks open.

And then, for some reason unknown to me, I walk toward them and follow them inside the apartment.

I clear my throat.

They both turn, Reid widening his eyes and Leif with a nondescript look on his handsome face.

"May we help you with something, Ms. Taylor?" Reid asks.

"I'm the freaking welcome wagon," I say.

Leif scoffs. "Could've fooled me." Then he softens. "I'm sorry."

I shrug. "Why are you sorry? I'm being a bitch."

A glance passes between them.

I know what it is.

They know what I've been through.

And they feel like they have to be soft for me. Treat me with kid gloves.

I get so damned uncomfortable when people are nice to me. It feels all wrong.

"You can agree with me," I say to Leif.

He glances at Reid. "Okay. I agree with you. You're being a bitch. But you have every right to be after what you've been through."

There he goes again, giving me an out. If a paperweight appeared in my hand at this moment, I'm pretty sure I'd hurl it right between his eyes.

Fine. They all want to say it's okay for me to act like this? Then I'll act like this.

I take in the beige walls and leather furniture in the living room. "This décor sucks."

I hate leather furniture.

We had leather furniture in our house growing up, and even though I know it's expensive and wears well and all that good crap, I still hate it, because it reminds me of home. Reminds me of my thighs sticking to it on a hot day.

It reminds me of my mother, sitting in her recliner and smoking a cigarette, and me, walking on eggshells, knowing she could snap at any moment.

"I think it looks fine," Leif says.

"Good," Reid says. "But if you want to change anything, go ahead. Just expense it."

"I'm easy," Leif says, giving me a stink eye. "I don't care much about décor."

"Good thing," I can't help saying. "Does everything have to be so neutral? And a glass-topped coffee table? Can't you people afford marble?"

Reid clears his throat. "This is a one-bedroom place," he

says to Leif, totally ignoring me, "and the bedroom is around that hallway, on the other side of the kitchen. The kitchen is fully stocked with groceries for you. And of course anything you need, just expense that as well."

"Must be nice," I scoff.

"Ms. Taylor, you have a credit card at your disposal for any necessities."

"I don't like to use it."

"That's funny," Reid says. "My assistant says you use it quite often."

I cross my arms. "I do. I said I don't *like* to. I hate not paying my own way."

"Then find a job," Leif says.

"I'm trying. But I don't have any education. Besides, Macy says I may not quite be ready."

"It's okay," Reid says, his voice gentle. "Macy has my confidence, and she knows what's best for you. We are all here for you, and we want you fully healed."

I scoff again. "Fully healed? Never going to happen."

"We know that." Reid reaches toward my shoulder and then appears to think better of trying to touch me. "A part of your experience will always be with you, but you can move forward with life. You're a smart girl, Ms. Taylor."

"I'm a woman."

"Of course." Reid attempts a smile, but I can see he's tense.

I seem to make everyone tense.

"I didn't mean to insult you," Reid continues. "You're a woman, a very intelligent woman, and my family is committed to helping you in any way we can."

Thank you, I say to myself.

I haven't said thank you to any of the Wolfes yet. The only people I've thanked are Macy and my doctors on the island.

But the Wolfes?

I just can't do it. Not yet. Even though I'm well aware of everything they've done for me.

I *am* grateful in my own way.

The words just don't seem to come out.

For some reason, I follow Reid and Leif into the bedroom.

The king-size bed, covered in a satin black comforter, draws my gaze. I like the décor better in here. A chest of drawers and a dresser line the wall, and a door is open to reveal a large walk-in closet. The apartment is the same layout as my own, only I have a queen-size bed.

"Looks top-notch," Leif says. "Thank you, Reid."

"Absolutely. No problem. Rock and I will feel a lot better with you this close to Kelly and the others."

"There are only three of us here right now," Kelly says.

"Some of the women chose to go straight home rather than stay here first." Reid cocks his head. "Jade, for example. Amethyst."

"They have names, you know." Of course, I don't know what they are.

"You're absolutely right. Carly. And Jenna."

"Why did they choose to go home?"

"They had family available. They wanted to go home to family."

Right. Family. I remember Katelyn—Moonstone—didn't want to go home because her mother was kind of a freak. Garnet—Aspen—seems to love her parents but wanted to stay here first, gather her bearings.

They're both gone now, married.

Aspen somehow snagged that other Navy SEAL guy, and boy, is he hot.

But damn... The one standing in front of me now? A hundred times hotter, and I've never liked blond men that much.

That's a strange thing, and something I was just talking to Macy about.

I'm finding men attractive again, which means I'm healing.

And Leif Ramsey is about the most attractive man I've ever laid eyes on.

Which means I need to get the hell out of here.

I turn.

"Kelly?"

I turn back around. I know Reid's voice, and that wasn't it.

It was Leif's voice that said my name.

"Yes?"

"I'm right next door. Whenever you need anything. That's what I'm here for. Anything."

I nod.

Then the words come out. The words I have such a hard time saying.

"Thank you."

7

LEIF

Once Kelly is gone, I turn back to Reid.

"My God..."

"I know, man. She is definitely a handful." Reid pulls a handkerchief out of his pocket and wipes his forehead. "Anything you need. Don't be afraid to ask or expense. We're determined to do right by Kelly."

"You know what her story is?"

Reid shakes his head. "Her therapy sessions are confidential. We get weekly reports from Macy but they only give us a bare minimum of information. She takes her doctor-patient confidentiality very seriously, as she should."

"I get the feeling she was a mess before the whole island thing," I say. "I met guys like her in the military. People who were fucked up before they got there. And man, we saw some fucked up things there, so I can't even imagine what it did to those guys."

"I doubt we'll find out anytime soon. She's not exactly a talker, as you've noticed."

"Except to be nasty," I say.

Reid nods. "Just be kind. That's my best advice."

"That hasn't done so well so far."

"No. But everyone deserves kindness, don't you think? Especially any woman who suffered at the hands of my father and that horrible island."

"Can I ask you a question?"

"Of course."

"Why did your family decide to keep the island? I never quite understood that."

Reid pauses a moment. "It's a valid question, and the four of us talked a lot about it. But it's prime real estate—"

I let out a chuckle. "You Wolfes. Always the businesspeople."

"True, but let me finish." He smiles. "Like I was saying, it's prime real estate, and we thought we could reverse what happened there, or at least make up for it. Spin lead into gold, so to speak. Riley was very adamant about building a retreat center not just for the women who suffered but for anyone else who needs help. Where better to recuperate than on a beautiful South Pacific island? It's also a great place for an artist retreat and colony, which was one of Roy and Charlie's dreams. Rock and I, of course, wanted something that would make money for business, so we came up with the Wolfe Resort and Casino."

"You have a lot of resorts and casinos in Vegas," I say. "Plus one in Reno and two in Atlantic City, as I recall."

He grins. "Doesn't mean I don't want more. But this one is going to be top-notch."

"And the others aren't?"

"You've been to our properties in Las Vegas," he says. "Like I told you at the meeting, we're opening soon. You,

Buck, Aspen. We want you to be our guests. After a week at that resort? You tell *me* if the others are top-notch."

I laugh, shaking my head. "It was a lucky day when Buck and I walked into your office, answering your call for security and investigation."

"Are you kidding me? We were the lucky ones that day. You two have been invaluable to us. I can't tell you how happy I am that Buck found love with one of my father's victims."

"Right? The two of them are amazing together. It's like they just fit, you know?"

"I do know. Zee and I are exactly like that." He glances at his watch. "Which reminds me, I have to get back. I promised Zee I'd be home at a reasonable hour tonight."

"You got it. Never take your woman for granted, Mr. Wolfe."

Reid wrinkles his brow. "Mr. Wolfe?"

"I don't know. It just seemed like a *Mr. Wolfe* moment. Give Zee my best, and little Nora."

"I will. Like I said, anything you need. Anything Kelly needs. You got it. No questions asked."

"Thank you for this opportunity."

He laughs then. "After a day with her, you're thanking me?"

"Hey, I know what it's like to deal with trauma. She's going to be okay, Reid. It's just going to take some time."

"I know. We won't rest until she's okay." Reid leaves the apartment, closing the door behind him.

These are some pretty nice digs, though I didn't expect anything different from the Wolfe family. I can't even imagine what the new resort on the island is going to be like. They certainly don't do anything halfway. I've been to the Wolfe resorts in Las Vegas, and they put the others to shame.

Funny.

I was actually planning to take a trip home to Texas right after Buck and Aspen's wedding, but this new assignment from the Wolfes takes precedence. I need to call my mom to let her know I'm not coming back. She won't be happy, but what can I say? Reid Wolfe is paying me bank for this. Plus, Buck just gave up his honeymoon for the same thing, so she'll understand.

I tap the phone and put it to my ear.

"Hello? Leif?"

"Hey, Mom," I say.

"How are you? Is everything okay?"

"I'm fine. Buck is fine, and the wedding went off great. But the Wolfes gave us a new assignment."

She sighs. "Which means you're not coming home as planned."

"I'm afraid not. But I will get home as soon as I can."

"I know you will, honey. Your father and I miss you a lot. So do your sisters."

"I know. Tell Laney and Scarlett I miss them. I'll be home as soon as I can. I'll be in touch."

"Okay, Leif. We love you."

"Love you too, Mom. Bye."

My dad is a rancher. He's pretty successful in Texas. But not as successful as our neighbors, the Bellamys. They're worth nearly a billion.

Someday, I'll probably go out and take over for Dad. When the kind of work I do here isn't feasible anymore. In other words, when I get too damned old and tired to do it.

But for now, I like it.

It keeps me fit. And I'm damned good at it.

I walk into the kitchen and open the door to the refrigerator. Reid wasn't lying. It is fully stocked with milk, eggs, bacon, all kinds of cold cuts—from the deli, not the grocery store—a loaf of bread, lots of fresh fruit, even some pudding cups.

I wander through the rest of the kitchen, opening cupboards and finding all the dry staples and a lot of canned goods as well.

In the freezer, I find a couple whole chickens, a bag of chicken breasts, several steaks, a couple pounds of ground beef, and a pork roast.

Too bad I'm not much of a cook.

Then my gaze falls on a book entitled *Cooking for Bachelors*.

I laugh out loud. Good old Reid.

He and Rock are great guys. How they came from someone as evil as Derek Wolfe is beyond me.

I take out the pork roast and set it to thaw in the sink. I have no clue how to make pork roast, but it can't be that difficult.

As I leave the kitchen, my doorbell rings, so I walk toward it and take a look through the peephole.

Then I open the door to greet Buck and Aspen.

"So, the new digs?" Buck says.

"Yep."

"Aspen and I are going to be staying here as well, but we have a two-bedroom suite on the eighth floor."

"Oh you do?" I raise my eyebrows. "Why, when you'll only be using one bedroom? Must pay to be married. What happened to the posh honeymoon suite at the Waldorf?"

Aspen smiles. "We can have our mini honeymoon here. It's actually really nice. We were wondering if you'd like to join us for dinner."

I gesture to the sink. "I just took a pork roast out of the freezer."

Aspen giggles.

"What?" I say.

She eyes the still-frozen roast. "Dinnertime is in a couple of hours. The roast won't even begin to thaw by then."

"For a guy who was raised on a ranch," Buck says, "you don't know shit about meat."

"I come from a very traditional household," I tell them. "My mom never let any men in the kitchen."

Aspen rolls her eyes. "You've got to be kidding me."

"I'm not. You'd actually like my mom. She's an amazing woman. Smartest woman I know and a hell of a cook."

"I'm sure she is," Aspen says. "But you need to learn how to take care of yourself."

"Reid left me a cookbook in the kitchen."

"Or you can just order takeout on the Wolfes' expense account," Buck says.

I laugh. "I'm sure I'll be doing my fair share of that as well."

"But tonight," Aspen says, "you're going to join us. Buck, who *can* cook, by the way, is making his mother's famous lasagna."

I narrow my eyes at Buck. "You cook? Other than putting melon on skewers?"

"I never told you that?"

"Nope. I guess we had other things to talk about in the trenches."

"Come up around seven thirty." Aspen shoves a stray lock of short hair behind her ear. "You know what? Come up around six. We'll have a glass of wine, talk."

"About what?"

"About how you and Buck screwed up my honeymoon." Her expression is stern, but then she laughs.

She's kidding.

Aspen is an amazing woman, and Buck is a lucky man.

Then something occurs to me. Like a lightbulb going off in my head.

"You mind if I bring a guest?"

"No. My lasagna is always enough to feed an army. Or the two of us." Buck laughs.

"I'm serious. What if I invited Kelly?"

Aspen drops her jaw. "Seriously?"

"She's a mess," I say. "She's not my idea of a good time either, but it's kind of what I'm paid to do. Make sure she's taken care of. I don't know, Aspen. Maybe you can get through to her."

"I don't even know her," Aspen says. "We didn't talk on the island. None of us did. Katelyn and I only got to know each other once we got here to New York."

"You said you and Katelyn used to watch TV while you were on the island."

"We did. That doesn't mean we talked. Katelyn and I and Onyx—I think her real name is Serena—used to watch old reruns in the common room. But we were rarely joined by any of the others."

"So you're saying you'd rather I not invite her?" I ask.

"I'm not saying that," Aspen says. "I feel for Kelly. I truly do. But she's...different. I mean. can you imagine? Being envious of the other girls when they were chosen instead of her? None of us wished any ill upon the other while we were there, but when we weren't chosen? It felt like a reprieve. There was no reason to get envious. There was plenty of reason to feel sorry for those who *were* chosen."

"My wife speaks the truth." Buck moves behind her and touches her shoulders.

"I know. But someone has to get through to this woman."

"She has Macy for that," Aspen says. "Your job is to make sure she's protected from Brindley or whoever's threatening her."

"Do you really think it's Brindley?" I ask.

"I don't know Brindley or Kelly," Aspen says. "From what I remember about Brindley, she seemed like a normal woman. She wasn't there for very long. Only a couple of months until we were rescued."

"Maybe I should talk to Brindley," I say.

"Maybe," Buck agrees. "But Aspen should go with you."

I point to my friend. "Why don't *you* come with me?"

"Because two big guys like us talking to a woman who was subjected to abuse and torture at the hands of other big men like us is not the best idea."

"Yeah, you're right. I should've thought of that." Buck's muscles are nearly as big as mine. Of course he'd say his are bigger.

"It's okay that you didn't," Aspen says. "You and Buck are such great guys, and you would never even think of hurting a woman. I'm sure it's difficult for you to understand that others live for that kind of shit."

"You're right." I let out a sigh. "All right, Aspen. Maybe we can talk to Brindley tomorrow. In the meantime... About Kelly and tonight?"

"Fine," Aspen says. "Invite her. My guess is she won't come anyway."

"She may not, but I've got to try."

"Good enough. We'll see you at six."

"Which apartment number on the eighth floor?"

"Apartment 810," Buck says. "See you in a few hours."

I shut the door behind them, head back in my kitchen, and replace the pork roast in the freezer. I glance at the cookbook and roll my eyes. No time for that now. Besides, my dinner is taken care of for tonight.

But first, I have to see Kelly.

And invite her to dinner.

8

KELLY

Sometimes time passes quickly.

Other times? Like today?

Every minute seems like an hour.

Because sometimes I don't feel like doing anything. I have a shelf full of books, and I used to like to read. Once my mother forbade me from playing volleyball with the other girls, I began to lose myself in books.

I read all the Little House books by Laura Ingalls Wilder, all of the Lemony Snicket books, all of the Harry Potters. Then I graduated to the Chronicles of Narnia by C.S. Lewis, and then young adult books. *Twilight* and its sequels, and whatever else I could find in the library.

I hid the books in the closet along with a flashlight. It gave me something to do for those hours on end when my mother locked me in. Eventually I managed to keep a jug of water in there as well, but I stopped that after a while. I could easily quench my thirst, but then I had to go to the bathroom, and that presented another problem when I was locked in the closet.

My shelf is full of amazing authors—some of the classics and some commercial fiction.

But today, none of them call to me.

Not even the trashy magazines sitting on my coffee table.

Today...I just feel...

I feel sorry for myself.

And angry with myself. Angry that I treated Leif and the others so badly today.

I always feel guilty afterward.

But I can't seem to stop doing it.

Macy says it's a defense mechanism. That I strike first before I can get struck myself.

She's right, of course. The therapists on the island said the same thing.

In fact, I think that's why they ultimately said I was ready to leave if I wanted to. Because I knew what my problem was.

I just haven't been able to fix it yet.

It's objective versus subjective.

Objectively, I know what my problem is and where it stems from.

Subjectively, though? That's another story altogether. It comes down to habit. Old habits are hard to break. But I have to break them. I have to if I want a life—and I desperately want a life, and to *live*.

I never felt suicidal, not ever. Not even on the island.

Not even when my mother was at her worst.

Macy asked me if I wanted to see my mother again...my answer was a resounding no.

I don't ever want to see that woman again.

I am curious though, whether she tried to find me when I went missing five years ago. Macy offered to look into it for me, but I told her not to.

First of all, I'm capable of looking into it myself. Reid Wolf has offered me any resources available.

But I don't want to.

The truth is? I'm afraid to.

I'm afraid what I'll find is that she never tried to look for me. That she didn't care that I disappeared off the face of the earth.

Why would she? I wasn't a daughter to her. I was simply a mouth to feed. Someone to treat horribly. To abuse. To make suffer. And then to pretend she did it all out of love for her only child.

What kind of a mother punches holes in her daughter's volleyball—that her daughter paid for herself—and gives it to her as a birthday gift?

What the hell kind of mother does that?

I bet Aspen's mother never did anything like that. Or Katelyn's. Or Lily's.

And that was far from the worst thing she did to me.

I try not to think about a lot of it, but it comes to me sometimes. Not in flashbacks or anything. Just images that force their way into the part of my mind I've tried to seal off.

I sigh, get off my couch, and walk to my bookshelf. I have to find—

I turn at the sound of a knock on my door.

It's someone who's already in the building, otherwise security would've called.

I look through my peephole.

Leif Ramsey.

Ex-Navy SEAL extraordinaire, and the most good-looking man I've ever seen in my short life.

"What do you want?" I demand through the door.

"I want to invite you to dinner," he says.

"I'm busy."

"I'm just going up to the eighth floor to have dinner with Buck and Aspen. They said I could invite you, and I'd like you to come. So would they."

I unlock my deadbolt and undo my chain. Then I open the door and face him. "That is a damned lie and we both know it."

"It's not."

I roll my eyes. "Neither of them wants to have dinner with me, and neither do you."

He doesn't reply, which tells me all I need to know.

"Look, I get that Reid Wolfe is paying you a fortune to watch over me, but I don't need a babysitter. I've said it before."

"This is dinner, Kelly." His tone is even and steady, a little firm. "Dinner. That's it."

"No, this is you trying to get to know me. Trying to figure out why I am the way I am."

Again, he doesn't reply.

Which again tells me everything I need to know.

"Is it such a crime to try to get to know you? I've been assigned to keep you safe. My job would be a lot easier if I knew you a little."

"Who says I want to make your job easy?"

He shakes his head and sighs. "Message received. Sorry I bothered you."

I go to shut the door, but my hands don't move. I step outside just as he's sliding his key card through his own door.

"Wait!"

He turns and looks at me. "What is it now?"

I pause a moment, biting my lip. "I'll go to dinner. I hate cooking anyway."

I'm not sure why I changed my mind. I do hate cooking, but I can easily order takeout.

"Good enough. I'll come get you at six."

"Okay."

Then I go back into my apartment and shut the door.

I'm not sure why I said yes. I'm also not sure why I said no in the first place.

I'm not really sure of anything anymore.

And that is my biggest problem.

9

LEIF

I stop myself from dropping my jaw when Kelly opens the door after my first knock.

Her auburn hair is down, falling in soft waves around her shoulders, and she's wearing a tight pink T-shirt and a black miniskirt with black tights and boots.

Not exactly what I was expecting.

"You ready?" I make myself say.

"Yeah." She grabs a black handbag from the table next to the door and joins me in the hallway.

Am I allowed to tell her she looks nice? Because she does. She's beautiful, even with her shitty attitude. I can't help but appreciate her loveliness. She has full pink lips, amazing blue eyes, and the longest eyelashes I've ever seen.

Maybe they're fake. Hell, I don't know. Whatever they are, they work for her.

Without talking, we walk to the elevator, where I hit the *up* button. It opens almost instantly, and I hold out my hand for her to precede me in. She looks at me kind of funny, but then she goes in, and I follow. I hit the button for the eighth floor, and the elevator's so quick, we're there almost instantly. We walk a few steps to apartment 810, and I knock.

Aspen opens the door, looking radiant as always with her short hair. She's also wearing a miniskirt. Hers is denim, and her legs are bare, although she's also wearing black boots.

"Leif, Kelly. Come on in." She holds the door open for us, letting her gaze rest on Kelly for a little longer than normal.

I inhale the robust scent of tomatoes and cheese. "It smells great in here."

"Do you like lasagna, Kelly?" Aspen asks.

Kelly nods but doesn't say anything yet.

"Good. Buck and I are having a glass of Chianti. What can I get the two of you?"

I defer to Kelly, glancing at her.

Kelly looks at each one of us. "Oh, am I supposed to respond first? I don't drink very much. Maybe I'll just start with some water."

"Absolutely. And you, Leif?"

"I'll try a glass of the wine."

In truth I prefer a good bourbon to wine, but hey, an Italian meal calls for Chianti.

Aspen leads us to the living room, which is a lot larger than mine. "Have a seat, you two. Buck is in the kitchen, and I'll be out with your drinks in just a minute."

Two glasses of wine already sit on the coffee table. Buck's and Aspen's, presumably.

I take a chair. Kelly takes another, leaving the couch for Aspen and Buck. She stares down at her lap, clasping her hands in front of her. She feels out of place, which is no surprise.

But part of me is glad she came. She's not drinking, so I can't depend on alcohol to open her up. That's not how I want her to open up anyway. If she's going to talk to me, I don't want it to be chemically induced. I think she has a rough story, and while I don't want to pry, knowing what she's been through will help me be able to protect her better. See to her safety.

Is it okay to tell her she looks nice tonight?

That's what I would say to any woman who looks nice.

So I clear my throat. "You look very nice tonight, Kelly."

She doesn't glance up at me, and she says nothing.

Okay... Perhaps not the best opener.

"Apparently Buck makes a great lasagna," I say. "He's Italian. His last name is Moreno."

Again, she doesn't look up, and she says nothing.

Lord, this is going to be a long night.

If I hadn't invited Kelly, I could be having a nice dinner with Buck and Aspen tonight. Instead, I have to think about every word I say and sit here watching a woman who is clearly uncomfortable and doesn't want to be here.

Why the hell did you say yes, then?

The words hover at the edge of my lips, but I won't say them. I'm a polite guy. I treat women with respect, even when they haven't earned it.

Kelly is the way she is for a reason, though. People don't become this harsh overnight. She's been through hell, but so has Aspen, and she's one of the nicest people I know.

But...Buck has told me her story, about how she nearly let revenge eat her alive.

So I need to give Kelly a break.

She deserves that much.

Aspen returns with a glass of wine for me and a glass of water for Kelly. Kelly mumbles her thanks and places it on a coaster on the small table between our two chairs.

Aspen takes a seat on the couch across from us, picks up one of the wineglasses, takes a sip, and then swirls the burgundy liquid in the glass. "I love a nice Chianti, don't you?"

Was that a question for me? I swirl the wine in my own glass and take a sip. It tastes like red wine. I'm no wine connoisseur. White wine tastes like white wine and red wine tastes like red wine.

"It's very good," I say.

"Buck will be out in a few minutes. He's putting the lasagna in the oven."

Oh, God, that's right. Aspen originally invited me at seven thirty, and then at six o'clock so we could talk.

It's going to be a freaking hour and a half before dinner is ready.

If Kelly doesn't start talking, that ninety minutes is going to seem like a year.

10

KELLY

My hands shake as I take a sip of my water.

Why did I agree to come here? Though I have to admit the lasagna smells good.

My mother used to make me spaghetti and meatballs every once in a while when I was a kid.

On her good days.

She would open a can of store-bought spaghetti sauce, form hamburger into tiny balls and fry them, and then pour it all over cooked spaghetti noodles.

It was my favorite meal, and I knew when I smelled spaghetti and meatballs that it was a good day for my mother. A day when I wouldn't end up in the closet.

She had a lot of good days after she took away my volleyball. For some reason that made her happy—to take away something that meant so much to me.

Macy says she needed me, and she was jealous of the volleyball. She thinks my mother suffered from something called borderline personality disorder. Probably combined with bipolar disorder. The two together are a difficult combination and require treatment most of the time.

But Macy can't be sure, of course, because she hasn't talked to my mother. Hasn't examined my mother. And she says my memories could be flawed.

Apparently, when you have a traumatizing childhood, your memories can't always be trusted. Even though I remember every single thing in Technicolor as if it were yesterday.

I sigh, which turns out to be a big mistake. Aspen and Buck both turn and stare at me.

"What?" I say.

"You sighed," Aspen says. "Is everything okay?"

Really? Did she just ask me that question?

"You know very well that everything is *not* okay," I say. "I'm being threatened. By Brindley."

"Yes, we know," Leif says, his voice measured. "That's why Buck and I are here. Did you know Buck and Aspen are missing their honeymoon to be here?"

I huff as I look around the living room. Leather furniture, of course, which I hate. It's not quite as colorless and drab as Leif's place, though. A few throw pillows in red and green make it look like Christmas. And the coffee table is dark wood without a glass top. So I don't risk breaking anything when I slam my hand onto it. "Well I'm sorry. I'm sorry that my safety made you miss your honeymoon."

I hate myself as soon as those words come out of my mouth. I'm not this person. But, as Macy says, how are these people supposed to know otherwise? They can't see inside my head. They only know what I say.

"I'm sorry." I force the words out of my mouth while purposefully refusing to rub my hand that smarts.

Aspen looks at me with wide eyes. "You are?"

"I said it, didn't I?"

God, here I go again.

"You know, Kelly," Leif says. "People would be nice to you if you were nicer to them. We're not your enemies."

"I shouldn't have come." I rise.

Aspen rises as well. "Please, sit down. Let's all try to get along. We're going to be spending a lot of time together, and as Leif said, I'm missing my honeymoon for this."

"I—"

Aspen gestures for me to be quiet. "I'm not saying that to make you feel guilty. Buck, Leif, and I all want to be here. We want to be here for you. I know what you've been through. I was there."

I open my mouth to retort but then shut it abruptly.

She doesn't know what I've been through. Sure, she was on the island. And Aspen went through hell on that island. I've heard the stories. She was a favorite to hunt, and she spent time in the infirmary. I don't know any of those details.

But she probably had an idyllic childhood. Two parents who loved and doted on her.

Plus, she's tall and strong and beautiful. The island didn't take that from her.

The island didn't take anything from me, either. My mother had already taken everything from me by the time I got there.

I sit back down. "All right. I'll stay." I take another sip of my water.

Buck joins us then, and I force myself not to gape at him. He's almost as good-looking as Leif, only dark where Leif is light. As much as I hate to admit it, he and Aspen make a stunning couple. Both dark-haired and dark-eyed, both tall and muscular. They'll have beautiful athletic children.

I take another sip of water. My throat hurts a little bit, and I'm not sure why.

Except I do know why. I spend my life choking back sobs so my throat is always constricted and in pain.

For once I'd like to be able to let it all go. Fly free, if only for moment.

"Everything smells great," Leif says.

"My mom's lasagna is the absolute best. Just ask Aspen. Every time we go to an Italian restaurant, I order lasagna and every time I say—"

"It's good, but nothing like my mother's," Aspen finishes for him, laughing.

Happiness radiates through both of them. I drop my gaze to Aspen's left hand, where her wedding set sparkles. It's got to be two carats for sure. A round solitaire set in a ring guard of diamond chips. Buck wears a plain gold band on his finger.

Again, I'm aware of the cloud of happiness that seems to enclose them. It's like a bubble of sunshine engulfing them, and some of it radiates onto Leif.

While I'm sitting in this chair below a gray cloud with rain threatening to fall.

Happiness is not an option for me. It never was.

Aspen sits on the couch, and Buck takes a seat beside her.

He grabs his glass of Chianti, swirls it, and then takes a sip. "This is one of my favorites. It's made in a tiny town in Tuscany, and I discovered it when Leif and I were living here last year. This little liquor store in the village stocks it, so of course I had to take Aspen there as soon as we got here, and I bought a case of it."

Aspen takes another sip of hers. "I have to admit that it's

one of the best Chiantis I've ever had. Not that I know a lot about wine. I just know what I like."

I have nothing to add to this conversation, so I say nothing.

"Are you a wine drinker, Kelly?" Aspen asks.

"Not really."

"Right, you said you don't drink much."

"Right," I reply.

"I'm a bourbon man myself," Leif offers. "But I like wine."

God, could this conversation get any duller?

Buck rises then. "Let me get the appetizers."

Thank God. Appetizers. We can chew instead of talk.

He walks to the kitchen and returns carrying a tray. "Antipasti," he says. "Or my version, anyway. These are skewers of dry salami, cantaloupe, green olives, and mozzarella drizzled with extra-virgin olive oil." He sets the tray on the coffee table, along with four plates stacked with napkins. "Help yourself."

I don't move.

Leif does. "You know me. You don't have to ask me twice." He grabs a plate, places two of the skewers on it and then takes a napkin. To my surprise, instead of keeping it for himself, he hands it to me. "Kelly?"

I'm too surprised not to take it. "Thank you," I murmur.

Then he smiles at me.

He smiles at me, and I feel...

I feel...something.

Something I've never felt.

I'm not sure what it is, but it's...pleasant.

It's just my body reacting to a good-looking man who did something nice for me. That's all it is.

But it's something.

And I have to say…I don't hate it.

I'm not sure how to eat these little skewers, so I wait until Aspen takes a bite. She picks up the small wooden skewer and bites the first piece off of it.

I do the same. The first piece is a small chunk of mozzarella cheese, and it's fantastic. The little bit of extra-virgin olive oil gives it a tang and it melts against my tastebuds.

The next bite is a salty olive, perfect after the cheese, and then the sweetness of a chunk of cantaloupe. That gives way to the umami of the salami. All bound together by extra-virgin olive oil.

"These are wonderful," I say.

A smile splits Buck's handsome face. "I'm so glad you like them. They're actually my own invention."

"They are?" Aspen raises her eyebrows.

"Yeah. Didn't I tell you that, baby?"

"You did not."

"Yeah. I love traditional antipasti, but it's a pain in the ass to eat it with your hands or with a fork and knife. So I invented my little antipasti skewers. You can put anything on them, but this combo is my favorite."

"I agree with Kelly," Leif says. "They're delicious."

"I've made these for you a hundred times, Phoenix." Buck laughs.

"You've made them once," Leif says. "And besides this, I didn't even know you could cook."

"Did he just call you Phoenix?" I ask.

"He did. It's my SEAL name." He smiles at me.

Which makes me uncomfortable.

"Are you from Phoenix?"

"No, I'm from a small ranching town in Texas. They called

me Phoenix in the Navy because I was able to get out of scrapes."

"Yeah, he's risen from the ashes more times than I can count," Buck says. "He had all our backs in Afghanistan. Phoenix here is a true hero."

"You both are." Aspen gazes adoringly at her husband.

Puke.

But I can't deny my respect for anyone in the military. I almost joined up myself after high school. My mother kicked me out of the house when I turned eighteen midway through my senior year. With no place to go, I was lucky to find a friend whose parents agreed to take me in until graduation. They didn't have to do that, and I'm eternally grateful.

I had no money for college, so the military seemed like a great choice. I took the test, passed the physical, and was ready to sign on the dotted line when a job came through. Waiting tables at a local establishment.

I should've gone with the military, but I let my insecurities make the decision for me.

It was easier not to leave. Easier to stay with what was familiar.

My friend's parents let me stay until I had enough money saved up from my job to rent a room from an elderly couple. I had my own entrance by way of the garage, so as long as I paid my rent, I didn't have any interaction with the Joneses.

I was angry, but I was forced to suppress that anger during work. To be friendly and keep a smile on my face at all times. That's how you get good tips when you're waiting tables. Most people don't care if you screw up every now and then as long as your attitude is good.

I found out I was a damned good server. I also found out I was damned good at suppressing my emotions.

"How's the job hunt going, Kelly?" Aspen asks.

Her voice jars me out of my thoughts.

"I'm not qualified for much except for waiting tables."

"There's an abundance of jobs in that area here in Manhattan," Buck says. "We have top-notch restaurants."

"Or you could talk to the Wolfes," Aspen says. "They helped Katelyn get a job. You know, Moonstone."

"They haven't made that offer to me," I say.

Then I wait.

I wait for the inevitable.

Because you don't deserve it.

Because you have nothing to offer their business.

They didn't make you that offer because you're being a bitch.

But silence reigns, until—

"I'll help you," Leif says. "We can go around tomorrow, check out the restaurants in the area, see if they're hiring."

I stop my jaw from dropping. "Why would you do that?"

"You're my project, Kelly."

Anger curls up my spine. "I'm no one's *project*," I grit out.

Leif raises his hands in mock surrender. "I don't mean it that way. I've been hired by the Wolfe family to keep you safe, so I'll go with you. Together, we can come up with something."

"Why would we come up with anything together?" I say snidely.

He smiles then. "Buck, back me up on this. You're a hard guy to say no to."

Buck lets out a guffaw. "You're so full of it, Phoenix."

Aspen is laughing as well, and she punches her husband good-naturedly on his upper arm. "You're pretty hard to say no to yourself."

Ugh. Sex vibes galore. The two of them are so in love it's pukeworthy.

Except...it's also kind of adorable. The sunshine of happiness that envelops them.

Part of me is envious.

Part of me knows I'll never have that, so why be envious?

Seems like I've spent my entire life envying others.

It's getting old.

"So what do you say, Kelly?" Leif continues. "First thing tomorrow, we go out. We'll find you employment."

"Do I have a choice in this?"

"Of course you have a choice. I'm not the boss of you."

"Right. You're just my personal bodyguard."

"If you choose to think of it that way," he says. "If I were you, I would choose to think of it as another person who has your wellbeing at heart and who wants to help."

God. I'm having such a hard time trying to dislike this guy. He's such a do-gooder.

"Fine," I relent. "Tomorrow, we go out together, and we look for a job for me. But I'm warning you. It's not going to be easy."

"I've always loved a challenge."

He smiles, and in that moment, a tiny bit of the ice around my heart melts.

11

LEIF

What the hell? I'm supposed to make sure she's safe, so I can't get out of spending time with her. This way, maybe I can help. This woman needs something in her life. I don't know if a job is the answer, but it can't hurt. Clearly she doesn't like being beholden to the Wolfe family. I can relate to that. I like standing on my own two feet as well.

She stays quiet while I talk with Buck and Aspen, and the time passes until finally the bell on the oven timer rings.

Buck rises. "That's my cue. Baby, get everyone situated at the table, and I will present my feast."

The table is a small oak rectangle in a dinette area off the living room and kitchen. I smile at the red-checkered table-cloth covering it.

Buck made it look like an Italian restaurant. All that's missing is a round bottle of Chianti in a wicker basket. Instead, the Chianti is in a regular wine bottle.

"Leif, why don't you take a seat?" Aspen nods. "And Kelly, sit beside him."

I hold out the chair for Kelly and she sits down. Then I take a seat next to her.

Buck first brings in a plate of garlic bread.

"Aspen wanted me to make a salad but I decided you should just enjoy my lasagna without being forced to eat something good for you." He laughs.

"Next time we have you over," Aspen says, "there *will* be a salad."

Kelly says nothing.

"Help yourself to some garlic bread, and I'll get the *pièce de résistance*." Buck heads back into the kitchen.

Aspen picks up the plate of garlic bread and hands it to me. I take a piece and give it to Kelly. She also takes a piece and hands it back to Aspen, murmuring her thanks.

Kelly murmurs when she's being nice. She shouts when she's being mean.

She's an interesting individual, and I'm intrigued by her. I may as well try to get to know her since I'm forced to be with her.

Forced proximity.

Fun.

At least she's nice to look at. She looks hotter than forty hells in that miniskirt, and her legs are shapely in the black tights.

"Here we are!" Buck strides in, strutting like a fucking peacock, carrying the lasagna while wearing red-and-white-checkered oven mitts.

I burst into laughter.

"What the fuck is so funny, Phoenix?"

"You are. You and your oven mitts."

"Would you rather I sear my hands on this hot casserole?"

"Sorry, man. It's just kind of hilarious."

"Why is it funny?" Kelly asks.

I turn and look at her. Her eyes are narrowed slightly. Is she serious? She's really asking me why this is funny?

"Buck is a Navy SEAL," I say. "We fought for our lives in Afghanistan, rescued people. And he's wearing oven mitts."

"And you find that funny?"

"I find that fucking hilarious," I laugh.

She cocks her head. Maybe she just doesn't get it, and that's okay.

"It's okay," Buck says to Kelly. "We've been giving each other shit since we first met."

Kelly nods slightly.

"It smells fantastic." I inhale. "Tomatoes, cheese, and lots and lots of meat."

"Don't forget the homemade pasta noodles," Buck says.

"You made homemade pasta?"

Buck laughs again. "Gotcha! My mom makes homemade pasta. I don't have that kind of time. Or the patience."

"I'm sure it will be delicious as always, honey." Aspen takes a seat.

"This casserole is hot." Buck sets it on the table. "Hence the oven mitts that Phoenix finds so humorous."

I choose not to make fun of Buck using the word "hence."

"But since it's so hot, just pass your plates to me, and I'll serve you." Buck nods to Kelly. "Ladies first."

Kelly's cheeks flush a beautiful pink as she hands him her plate. "Just a small piece, please."

"You got it." Buck puts a massive piece on her plate.

"That's a small piece?" she asks.

"Yeah. If you're Italian." Buck puts the same-size piece on Aspen's plate. "Here you go, baby."

"Hey, I didn't ask for small piece."

"Don't you worry your pretty head. There's plenty more where that came from."

I hand Buck my plate. "I'll have a fucking giant piece."

"You got it, Phoenix." He slaps a huge portion onto my plate, nearly knocking the slice of garlic bread off the side of it. I set my plate back down in front of me and inhale again.

Robust Italian food. Good stuff.

When you grow up with a Norwegian mother, you get a lot of lutefisk and lefse. It's good, but there's nothing like good old southern Italian cuisine.

"Dig in." Buck unfolds his napkin and places it across his lap.

I cut off a small piece of lasagna with my fork and bring it to my mouth. I blow on it and then slide it between my lips.

Damn. Buck can cook. I swallow against the heat of lasagna. "How is it that I've never had this before?"

"The ingredients weren't readily available in the trenches of Afghanistan."

I put my fork down and make a face at Buck. "I mean since we've been back, dickhead. I've had your antipasti but not this."

Kelly stiffens beside me. Is she offended that I called Buck a dickhead? Hell, we've called each other worse.

"I don't know. The antipasti takes about thirty seconds to put together. Other than that, I haven't done a lot of cooking. You and I have been going from one place to another working for the Wolfes. But since Aspen and I can't have our honeymoon, I want us to at least have a good home-cooked meal."

"It's delicious. Even your garlic bread is delicious."

"Thanks, Phoenix. But I've got to be honest. All of this is nothing compared to what my mom can do."

Aspen nods and swallows her bite of food. "When Buck

first took me to meet his parents, after Luke and Katelyn got married, Marina made lasagna. I swear to God, it was like heaven on a plate."

Kelly stiffens again.

"You okay?" I ask.

She chews the lasagna and swallows. "Yeah. Why?"

"You just seem...tense."

Which is an understatement. The tension is flowing off her in waves, and I sensed it get stronger when Buck mentioned his mother.

"I'm fine." She takes another piece of lasagna with her fork and shoves it inside her mouth.

"My mom's a good cook," Aspen continues, "but nothing like Buck's mom. She should be a chef. She could open her own Italian restaurant."

"My mom doesn't want to work that hard," Buck laughs.

"But she could make it big," Aspen says. "Her cooking is the best Italian food I've ever had."

"She wouldn't trust anyone to do any of it," Buck says. "She wouldn't hire a chef. She'd want to be the chef. And she would never take any time off, because she wouldn't trust any other chef to do it right."

"I agree with Aspen," I say. "This lasagna is the best I've tasted. By the way, how come you never took me home to dinner?"

"Because, Phoenix, you're not nearly as pretty as Aspen is."

I laugh. Buck and I will give each other three shades of shit all night. It's part of how we cope. We're good friends, of course, but we also have the same horrendous memories from our time on duty. From the scrapes we got out of. And one where we barely made it out alive. We both have the scars to prove it.

So we give each other shit. We laugh. We enjoy life. Because we understand what a gift life is. That's why Aspen is so good for Buck. She understands that life is a gift. Those women were lucky to escape with their lives, and they all have the scars to prove it as well.

Buck told me a bit of what happened to Aspen over there, but there's a lot he doesn't talk about, and I certainly won't force it. Those are Aspen's stories to tell, not his. Suffice it to say that Buck says what Aspen went through was nearly as bad as what we went through or worse. I'd say worse, for sure, because we signed up and knew what the possibilities were. The women did not.

And beside me sits Kelly. Kelly, who doesn't seem at all grateful for the second chance she's been given.

Every once in a while, a shred of humanity seems to shine through her. But most of the time, she's been shut off. She's built a big brick wall around herself, and I understand why. It's tempting, when you've been through something unspeakable, to wall yourself off and never feel again. Buck and I both struggled with that when we came home.

But it doesn't help. In the short term, maybe it numbs the hurt, but in the long term? It's no way to live.

I'm not a therapist. I can't help Kelly in that way. She's on her own. She has to recapture the joy of life. I wish I could help her, but I can't.

The beauty of Buck's delicious meal—other than deliciousness itself—is that we don't have to make much conversation. We're too busy eating. I clean my plate like a pro and take a second helping.

Kelly cocks her head at me. "Are you a bottomless pit or something?"

"Yep. And damned proud of it."

"How can you eat so much?"

"I exercise a lot. I expend a lot of energy and calories. Buck and I both do. When we were overseas, we ate about six thousand calories a day. That's when we could get food, of course. These days, I eat around three thousand calories a day."

"What do you mean, when you could get food?" she asks.

"We were in a third-world country, Kelly. There wasn't always food available."

"Yeah, and those MREs get old pretty fast," Buck says.

"MREs?" Kelly says.

"Meal, ready-to-eat. That's what it stands for," I explain. "All processed stuff that's vacuum sealed against every microbe. Sounds delicious, right?"

"You guys are big. Surely they gave you enough calories in your MREs."

"Yeah, they tried anyway. And we ate it because we had no other choice. But there were times..."

"Don't go there, bud," Buck says.

I clear my throat. "Suffice it to say, there were times when we didn't have access to food. So we made do."

Kelly says nothing further.

12

KELLY

Something is happening to me that I don't quite understand.

I have questions. Lots of questions that I want to ask Leif about his time overseas and as a SEAL. About not having enough to eat. About needing six thousand calories a day.

So many questions...

And the weirdest thing is? I haven't been this curious in a long time. I can't remember the last time I wanted to ask someone this many questions.

I ask Macy a lot of questions during our sessions, but they all concern me. Sometimes they're about my mother, but mostly about me and my life.

Here sits a man I barely know, and I have all these questions about his life.

I won't ask, though. First, I'm not comfortable asking, but more importantly, Buck told him not to go there.

What does that mean?

They were in the military—Navy SEALs, which means that they were the best of the best.

Which also means...they probably saw and experienced some hell.

If I had gone into the military instead of taking that serving job after graduation, would I have had those experiences? Added to the horrendous life I'd already led?

On the other hand...perhaps my life would be better. I wouldn't have been in combat, but I might have been sent overseas.

But the biggest reason? During my fifth year at the restaurant, I was taken.

If I'd been in the military, I wouldn't have been at the restaurant, and maybe I wouldn't have been taken to that horrible island.

Before I know it, the huge portion of lasagna Buck served me is gone. It was delicious. The best meal I've had in some time.

We were fed very well on the island. A lot of seafood, though, which isn't my favorite, but I learned to get it down because it was all that we had. We weren't starved on the island by any means. No, we needed to be strong because the men who hunted us wanted worthy prey.

The only time I've been starved was during my childhood. When I lived with my mother. The only time I knew hunger, and I don't ever want to know it again.

"So you liked it, I guess." Leif gazes down at my clean plate.

"I did. Thank you, Buck."

Buck smiles. "You're very welcome, Kelly. Aspen and I would love to have you dine with us again sometime."

Again, I resist dropping my jaw.

Why are these people being nice to me?

It's an easy question to answer.

Because Reid Wolfe is paying them.

Always an ulterior motive.

No one is nice to me unless they have to be.

"Would you like some more?" Aspen asks.

"No, thank you. This was more than enough."

"You sure? Buck made enough to feed an army... Or should I say navy." She smiles as she traces her hand over Buck's arm.

What the hell? It was delicious, and I wouldn't mind a little more. "Maybe just a bit."

Then I do something I haven't done in a while.

I attempt to move my lips upward. I attempt to smile.

I'm not sure if I'm successful. God, when was the last time I smiled?

Maybe a better question would be... When was the last time I had something to smile about?

I get no reaction from anyone at the table, so my attempt to smile was clearly unsuccessful. Perhaps my facial muscles don't even move that way anymore.

Buck takes my plate, cuts me the small portion I wanted in the first place, and hands the plate back to me.

"Thank you," I mumble.

Leif is still working on his second heaping plateful, using his garlic bread to wipe up the sauce. "Fucking awesome," he says with his mouth full.

Ugh. I hate when people talk with their mouths full. Maybe it's because my mom used to smack me when I did it, so I quickly learned not to do it.

Though it's rude, I don't think Leif is a rude person. It's more likely that he's enjoying the food that much.

I dig into my second portion of lasagna, which is the best meal I've eaten in a long time.

I don't cook for myself often. I was forced to do it when I was too young to be using a stove, and I got pretty good at scrounging around the house to make something edible for dinner to feed my mother and me when she refused to cook.

Sometimes it was hot dogs. Sometimes it was a box of macaroni and cheese. Sometimes it was plain pasta or simple peanut butter and jelly sandwiches. On good days, I found hamburger in the house. I learned how to make almost anything out of hamburger.

But to be able to cook like this? Prepare something that rivals anything I've eaten in a restaurant? He's one talented man.

Aspen is a lucky woman.

I should tell her that. I should be happy for her.

I can't, though. Why am I always so envious of everyone else?

Macy says it's because my life has been troubled and I'm so insecure that I can't help but be envious. She says it will take time, and I *have* gotten better.

I'm trying to focus on the gratitude. I'm grateful to be alive. No matter how bad my life got—either with my mother or on the island—I never wanted to end my life. Macy says that's wonderful, that I have a zest for life, and I can be happy. It's a choice.

Leif finally cleans the second plate and is conversing with Buck and Aspen about their honeymoon that was delayed.

Delayed because of me.

I have nothing to add to the conversation, so I finish up my second portion of lasagna and then simply sit. Quietly.

They continue until Aspen rises. "I know you're all full,

but I do have some berries and whipped cream for dessert. I wanted something light. Kelly, do you like fresh berries?"

"Sure."

"Great! I'll be right back."

She heads into the kitchen while Buck and Leif continue their conversation.

"Obviously Aspen didn't want to go to Hawaii or anywhere else in the South Pacific," Buck is saying, "so we decided on Florida. Miami Beach."

"Did Reid set you up at a resort?"

Buck smiles. "He did. Good thing, too, because we were able to change our reservations when we needed to."

I feel the gazes upon me, like lasers from their eyes boring holes into my flesh.

"You might as well say it," I say.

Leif turns to me. "Say what?"

"That it's my fault. It's my fault that Aspen and Buck aren't on their honeymoon right now."

Buck wrinkles his forehead. "No one's saying that. Weren't you listening to our conversation?"

"You didn't say it in words."

"Listen," Leif says. "I can tell you this about Buck. If he has something to say to you, he will never mince words."

"And you?" I raise my eyebrows.

"I won't be mincing words with you either, Kelly. That I can promise you."

"No one is blaming you for Aspen and me missing our honeymoon," Buck says. "We were just talking *about* the honeymoon. About where we decided to go and why."

"You think I don't know what subtext is?"

"Oh my God." Leif shakes his head. "You're a piece of work, you know that?"

"What's that supposed to mean?" I snap.

"I don't know. Why don't you tell me what the *subtext* is?" His jaw is clenched.

Buck rises then. "I think I'm going to help Aspen." He disappears into the kitchen.

"I suppose he couldn't wait to get the hell away from us," I say.

"Buck and I have been friends for years," Leif says. "I'm pretty sure he couldn't wait to get away from *you*."

His words cut through me.

I've hardened myself so much over the years, ever since I was a child, and very few things actually hurt me.

What Leif just said did. So much so that I feel myself wincing.

"We're here to help you," Leif continues. "I don't know how many times I have to say it."

"You're being paid very handsomely to help me."

"So what? I'm a Navy SEAL. So is Buck. We don't do anything half-assed, whether we're paid to or not. So we are here to help you, and God damn it, I'm going to help you." He shakes his head. "Even if it fucking kills me in the process."

"I never asked for your help."

"No, you didn't. But Reid asked me to help. I owe Reid a lot, so I will do as he asks."

"Because he's paying a lot of money."

He raises his hands in the air. "What do you want me to say, Kelly? That I'm happy to take his money? Newsflash, I am. The Wolfe family pays Buck and me very well for what we do for them, and we earn every penny of it. Especially in this case," he mumbles.

"I heard that."

"Good. Then you won't worry about having to interpret

the *subtext*." He rolls his eyes. "There's no fucking subtext, Kelly. I say what I mean."

I open my mouth to speak, but Aspen and Buck return, she holding a tray filled with four dessert bowls full of berries topped with whipped cream.

"Dessert is served," she says, a bit tentatively.

Leif smiles—a gorgeous smile—as if nothing just happened between us. "I am so looking forward to it, Aspen."

13

LEIF

We get a short reprieve after dessert when Kelly excuses herself to use the bathroom.

"My God, Phoenix." Buck shakes his head. "I don't envy you."

"She's a piranha," I agree. "So is it wrong that I think she's the most beautiful woman I've seen in a long time?"

"Kelly *is* a beautiful woman," Aspen says. "Every woman on the island was. Beautiful and strong." She grimaces. "Worthy prey."

"Reid's not paying you enough," Buck says.

"You're telling me. *Subtext.*" I rub my forehead, trying to ease the tension. "She'll find out soon enough that I'm not a subtext kind of guy."

Buck laughs then. "No, you're certainly not."

"You know," Aspen says, "it's funny. None of us really knew each other on the island. We were too busy trying to deal with our own lives. We couldn't get involved in each other's. Kelly was a little different in that respect."

"Right. You say she got jealous."

"Yeah, and I'll never understand why. I was one of the more popular women on the island. Big strong men wanted to take down the athlete."

Buck takes his wife's hand. "You okay, baby?"

"Yeah. I can talk about it now. You and I have been through a lot of therapy, and I'm finally in charge of my anger. I was totally out for revenge, right Buck?"

Buck pats Aspen's hand. "She was. But she's settled down now."

"Maybe you should talk to Kelly, Aspen." I say. "She sure as hell has an anger problem."

"But I don't get the feeling that hers is bent on vengeance," Aspen says. "It's something else with Kelly. Something I can't put my finger on."

I sigh. "So you won't talk to her then?"

"I'm happy to talk to her," Aspen says. "But talking is a two-way street. Talking *at* her won't do any good. She needs to be receptive."

"Do you know why she was called Opal?" I ask.

Aspen wrinkles her brow. "I have no idea. Opals are white or bluish tinted. Maybe her eyes. Kelly has reddish hair and blue eyes."

"You're forgetting about the fiery opal, baby," Buck says.

"There's a fiery opal?" I ask.

"Yeah. Don't you know anything?"

"I'm not a student of gemstones," I say to them. "But you are?"

"Yeah, did you know that?" Buck erupts in laughter. "I don't know shit about gemstones, but my mother was born in October, and the opal is the birthstone for that month. She has several opal pieces of jewelry, and one is a fiery opal. They're rare and expensive. But they're gorgeous. They look kind of like a regular opal, but instead of reflecting white or blue, they reflect this fiery orange."

Aspen rolls her eyes. "I doubt anyone put that much thought into it. Some of us had reasons for being named what we were. I have that strawberry angioma birthmark. Katelyn has porcelain skin and light blue eyes, like a moonstone. Onyx had really dark eyes, almost black. Jade had green eyes. Amethyst had blue eyes, so that made no sense. Lily is of Indian descent, with darker skin and eyes, so how does Tiger Eye make sense? There was nothing red about Ruby. She was black with very dark skin. And Turquoise had brown eyes. They didn't all make sense. Opal doesn't make sense for Kelly."

"It doesn't?"

Kelly stands in the entryway to the dining room.

"Hey," I say.

"Don't try to deny it. I know you were talking about me."

"Who's denying anything?" I ask.

She walks in slowly. "I don't appreciate you talking about me."

"Then be a nicer person," I say. "And you'll give us no reason to talk about you. Besides, we were only talking about the gemstone names."

She huffs. "I'm ready to go."

"I'm not."

"Fine. I'll go down to my apartment by myself."

"Be my guest."

Except Aspen and Buck are glaring at me.

I rise. "Fine. I'll go with her. Then I'm coming right back here."

"Actually," Buck says, glancing at his wife. "Dinner is over. Aspen and I have an...appointment."

Great. The newlyweds want to go to bed. I can't blame Buck. He should be on his honeymoon.

"Message received. See?" I say to Kelly. "*That* is subtext. They want to go to bed."

She scoffs but then turns to Aspen and Buck. "Thank you for inviting me. I really did enjoy the lasagna."

What? Did I just enter the Twilight Zone? How many personalities does this woman have?

"You are welcome here anytime," Aspen says, smiling.

"Except for right now," I clarify. "The two of them have an *appointment*."

Buck laughs. "Phoenix, would you get the hell out of here, please?"

I follow Kelly to the door, and Aspen gives me a hug. "Thanks for coming."

Then she does something unexpected.

She pulls Kelly into an embrace.

Kelly keeps her arms straight at her sides, but at least she doesn't pull away.

"Thank you for coming," Aspen says.

We leave their apartment and walk to the elevator.

Seconds later, we're back on the fourth floor, heading to our respective apartments. I walk Kelly to her door and hold out my hand to take her key.

"I'm perfectly capable of opening my own door." She slides the key through the reader and the door clicks open.

When she doesn't go in right away, I raise my eyebrows.

"Did you need something?"

She shrugs. "You guys were talking about me. I heard some of it. You don't have any idea what I've been through. You don't know my story." She looks at the floor.

"I'm willing to listen if you want to tell me your story."

"Why would you be willing to listen to me? I've treated you badly."

"Yeah, you have."

"I guess you're just a glutton for punishment." She still doesn't close the door.

"What do you need, Kelly? I'm here for you. Tell me what you need."

"I need to be left alone. I need to heal in my own way. I need you to get Brindley to stop stalking me. Threatening me."

"We don't have any evidence that it's Brindley, and she denied everything."

"Of course she denied everything. You think she's just going to admit what she's been doing? Breaking the law? Stalking someone?"

"But you said she admitted it."

"She did." Kelly balls her hands into fists. "I mean, she all but admitted it. I could tell by her tone."

I can't help myself. "From *subtext?*"

"Damn it!" Kelly plows her fist into the wall. "What good are you if—"

I grab her then.

I can't take anymore of her chatter.

So I shut her up the only way I know how.

I crush my mouth to hers.

14

KELLY

I should push him away.

Why is he kissing me, anyway? The man obviously hates me.

But my God, when was the last time I was kissed?

Have I ever been kissed this way? This passionately? By someone this good-looking?

I grip his shoulders, ready to yank myself away from him, but instead, I melt into him and part my lips.

A low growl emanates from him, and he sweeps his tongue into my mouth.

He tastes of tomatoes, garlic, a tiny tinge of sweetness from the whipped cream and berries.

My God, it's the most intoxicating flavor ever. Who knew kissing someone who tastes like garlic could be so amazing?

I shouldn't be doing this.

He works for the Wolfe family, and he's supposed to protect me.

But my God...

I let my tongue slide into his mouth as I deepen the kiss.

Another growl from him.

But then—

He breaks the kiss with a loud smack. Pulls away from me. Presses his back against the wall of the hallway and closes his eyes. "Fuck. I'm sorry."

"Yeah, that's pretty much what I figured."

He opens his eyes then. "Hey, you kissed me back."

"It was...instinct. Pure and simple."

"That what you're calling it these days?"

I whip my hands to my hips. "What the hell is *that* supposed to mean?"

"It means, Kelly, that you kissed me back. Maybe it was a mistake for me to kiss you, but you could've stopped it. You could've pushed me away, and you didn't. So if there's a mistake here, it was made by both of us."

My instinct is to fight him. Tell him he's wrong.

But he's not wrong.

I *did* kiss him back.

I liked it.

I liked it a lot.

I swipe the back of my hand across my lips, trying to wipe Leif from me.

My lips are tingling, as if warm blood is flowing to them for the first time in...forever maybe.

We didn't kiss on the island. The men weren't interested in that, and we certainly weren't interested in kissing them.

And the truth of the matter? I've only dated a few men in my life. My mother didn't allow me to have dates when I was living at home. For the five years I lived in an apartment and waited tables, I dated a few men. Kissed a few men. Slept with a few men.

But that kiss that Leif and I just shared?

It was more exciting than going to bed with any of the men from my past.

Macy says a lot of the women from the island are afraid to feel.

Feeling has never been my problem. My problem, she says, is that I focus too much on the *negative* feelings.

Anger, envy, jealousy.

If I can refocus that into the positive emotions, I'll be a happier person.

The only problem is? I don't know what *happy* feels like. The closest I came were the five years between high school and my abduction, when I worked my ass off waiting tables and lived paycheck-to-paycheck in a small apartment I could barely afford.

It was better than living with my mother for sure, and better than living in my friend's home and feeling beholden. But life was hard.

Happiness seemed to be a luxury that I didn't have enough time for.

"Go in," Leif says. "I won't leave until I know you're safely inside with your doors locked."

I don't move, though. My door has relocked, and I need to slide the card again. I reach for it, but Leif takes it from me, slides it through. The lock clicks, and he opens the door, gesturing for me to go in.

And all I can think about is how much I want to kiss him again.

"Most of the restaurants in the area open around nine to get ready for the lunch crowd and then the dinner crowd. I'll be by to pick you up at nine thirty, and we'll see about finding you a job." He rakes his gaze over me. "Wear something a little more conservative. Black pants and a blouse if you have it." Then he closes the door, and it clicks locked.

I stand, my back against my door, and slide into a squatting position.

Still feeling his lips on mine.

15

LEIF

Once inside my apartment, I rake my fingers through my hair and flop onto my couch.

My dick is still throbbing inside my jeans.

What the hell was I thinking? Kissing Kelly? That's the last thing she needs. I sure as hell don't need it either.

The woman has issues—serious issues—and I can't interfere with her healing. I'm here to protect her. To help her. To see that no harm comes to her.

I can't *be* that harm.

But damn...

Her lips are so full and soft, her tongue like crushed velvet.

Her body felt so good against mine. And now? All I can think about is what she might look like naked. That gorgeous fair skin, her plump tits, her round ass. Her shapely legs wrapped around me.

And she, looking down at me through those heavily lidded blue eyes.

Fuck.

Buck and Aspen are up in their place, screwing like bunnies.

Damn it all to hell.

I rise, head to my bedroom, take a shower, and take care of what I'd like to be taking care of inside Kelly.

Then, after toweling off, I fall into bed, naked. Morning will come early, and I'm going to need a good strong workout. I need a lot of release before I can deal with Kelly again.

~

I ONLY KNOCK ONCE, and Kelly opens the door to her apartment.

I resist the urge to suck in a breath.

She looks—in a word—spectacular.

Her gorgeous auburn hair is swept up into a high ponytail, and she's wearing a light-purple blouse and black dress pants, as I suggested. On her feet are black leather slides. Good. I was afraid she'd wear high-heeled sandals or boots, and we'll be doing a good amount of walking today.

Since I told her what to wear, I figured I shouldn't show up in jeans and a T-shirt, so I'm also wearing black pants, black leather dress shoes, and a white button-down, no tie.

I try not to gape at her, but damn, she looks good. Almost as good as she looked in that miniskirt last night.

Kelly cleans up nice, and whether she's going for professional or sultry, she can pull it off.

I hate to think of her this way, but it's very clear why she was chosen to go to the island. Every woman I've met from that damned island is picture-perfect to look at, and Kelly is certainly no exception.

Again, I wonder about her naked body. What kind of scars she might have.

Because all of the women have scars—the kind that can and can't be seen.

I will never see Kelly naked. The kiss was a mistake, and that's my first order of business this morning.

To apologize.

"Before we go," I say, "I need to apologize for last night."

"Yeah, you really should."

She's determined not to make this easy. "I truly am sorry. I overstepped my boundaries, and it won't happen again." I check my watch. "Are you ready to go? I made a list of some restaurants in the area that are hiring."

She walks out the door, carrying a small black purse, and closes it behind her. "Yes, I'm ready."

"Good." I gesture for her to lead and we walk to the elevator.

Our first stop is a delicatessen about a block away.

"Seriously?" She scoffs. "You want me to work at a deli?"

"They're looking for servers. You won't be slicing meat or making sandwiches. You'll be serving."

"I can't make any money there."

"Are you kidding me?" I gesture toward the front window. "Do you know how many seatings they have at this place? You'll make plenty of money, and if you're good, your tips will be great."

"Fine." She huffs and opens the door.

Even at ten in the morning, the deli is hopping. They do a huge breakfast and lunch business, according to my research. But already I see that this place is a mistake. It's jam-packed, with people yelling orders behind the counter, and I have no idea who's in charge.

So I grab Kelly's arm and escort her back out.

"Excuse me?" she says.

"I agree with you. This is not the best place for you. We'll be sitting around forever before we find someone to talk to you."

"Good. I don't want to work in a deli."

"Well, you're in luck. The next restaurant is called The Glass House. It's one of the best restaurants in Manhattan, and they're looking for servers."

Her eyes widen. "The best restaurant in Manhattan?"

"One of the best," I say.

"I... Leif, I worked at a diner in Phoenix. I'm not qualified to work at the best restaurant in Manhattan."

"*One of* the best," I clarify again, "and if you've worked at a diner, then you're good on your feet, you're quick, and you can keep lots of orders in your head at once. You can work anywhere."

"But Leif..."

The sound of my name from her lips gives me a jolt. The kind of jolt I really don't need around her. The kind that makes me want to do things she's clearly not ready for.

"Hey," I say. "It's my job to help you. I'm not going to steer you wrong. Trust me."

She scoffs.

I roll my eyes.

That sweet attitude was bound to be gone after a second or two.

"Why should I trust you?"

"That's your prerogative. You don't have to trust me. But the military trusted me. Buck trusted me. The citizens of this great country trusted me and all the other military men and women to keep them safe. But I don't know, Kelly. Why should *you* trust me?"

She opens her mouth.

Yep, here it comes. More acidic words from this beautiful woman.

"You think I could do it? Wait on tables at a fine restaurant?"

Color me surprised. My jaw drops, but I close my mouth quickly to reply. "Absolutely. You worked at the diner for what? Five years?"

She nods.

"How did you do there? Were your customers happy?"

"If they hadn't been, I would've been fired."

"There you go, then. You look great this morning. Just keep your air of professionalism, and you're going to be fine."

She bites her bottom lip, and then she nods. "Okay."

I open my mouth to give her a smartass comment, but I restrain myself. When she has these tiny sparks of niceness, I shouldn't do anything to make them stop.

We walk a block, not talking, until The Glass House appears. The building is red brick and unassuming. I open the door for her, and she walks ahead of me.

She gawks. Here's where unassuming ends. The host's station is dark wood with ornate carvings, and beyond, the dining room is lavish with secluded booths lining the walls and round tables throughout.

"I..."

"Ask for the manager in charge of hiring," I tell her, giving her a subtle push. "Relax. You're going to do great."

"You mean... You're not coming with me?"

"I'm not looking for a job. How do you think it would look if you brought someone with you to apply for a job?"

"Fine," she harrumphs. "If you don't want to help me, you don't have to."

"Oh my God." I inhale deeply, practicing patience. "You know I can't go with you. I'm going to stand right here by the door, and I will wait. They will either say yes, a manager will see you, or no, there aren't any jobs available. Whatever happens, whether you talk to someone or not, I will be here when you're done. If you don't end up with a job, we'll go to the next place."

"I'm not a moron, Leif. I know how this works."

"Then you know it won't look good if I go with you."

She nods then. Draws in a breath. Advances toward the door.

16

KELLY

My nerves are jumping under my skin, but I draw in another breath slowly and exhale. Then I try —I *really* try—to smile.

"May I help you?" A thin gentleman behind the podium asks.

"Yes, thank you. Is a manager available?"

"Linda is here. May I ask what this is regarding?"

"Yes, of course. I understand that the restaurant is looking for servers. I'd like to speak to Linda about the possibility of employment."

"Yes, we are. She's talking to someone else at the moment, but I'll let her know you're waiting if you'd like to have a seat." He gestures to the bench where Leif is already sitting.

I smile again—or try to. "Thank you very much. I'm happy to wait."

"Could I get your name?"

"Yes, of course. It's Kelly. Kelly Taylor."

The young man makes a note on a Post-it, and then he

leaves the podium. I head to the bench and sit down next to Leif.

"So?" he says.

"The manager's talking to someone else right now. She'll get to me in a minute." I frown.

"Great."

"What's great about it? Someone beat me here. The person who's here is going to get the job, and I won't."

"Oh my God." Leif rubs his forehead. "You are going to be the death of me, Kelly."

"No one's forcing you to be here."

He doesn't reply. Just shakes his head, sighing.

I sit, clasp my hands in my lap, trying to ease the shivers. Already I have goosebumps on my forearms. This place is as fancy as Versailles. Not that I've ever been to France, but I've seen photos. I got a look at a crystal chandelier when I was talking to the host.

I check my watch every couple of seconds. Check my emails on my phone. Even attempt to play *Candy Crush*.

Nothing soothes my nerves.

After what seems like hours, an attractive woman with blond hair walks toward me. "Are you Kelly?"

I rise. "Yes, I am."

"I'm Linda Parker." She holds out her hand. "It's great to meet you. Come with me, and we'll talk about the server position."

I attempt to smile once more. I want to look to Leif for reassurance, but I force myself not to. I go with Linda, and she leads me to a table in the dining room near the back.

"Please, have a seat."

I take a seat.

"Would you like some coffee? Water?"

"Thank you. A glass of water would be nice."

"Of course." She signals to a busboy setting tables.

He comes right over.

"Could we get a couple waters, please?"

"Sure thing, Linda." He waves and walks away.

"So, Kelly," Linda says. "Tell me what kind of experience you have serving."

"I'm originally from Phoenix, and I was a waitress at the Junction Diner for five years."

"Any experience in a fine restaurant?" Linda glances at her tablet.

"No, but I'm certain I can do the job. I'm great on my feet, and my customers were always satisfied."

"What made you leave Phoenix?" Linda asks.

Oh, God. I should've thought about what to say. And now I have no clue. Should I tell the truth?

"It...wasn't by my choice." I look down.

Then I draw in a breath, trying to gather what little courage I have and resisting the urge to come out fighting.

I meet Linda's gaze. "This isn't something I like to talk about, Linda, but I was abducted from my restaurant in Phoenix. I was held captive on Derek Wolfe's island for five years."

Linda's eyes widen. "Oh my God, I'm so sorry. I shouldn't have asked that question."

No, you should have known. Those are the words I want to spew in her face. But instead—

"You didn't do anything wrong. It's a valid question. But I want to be truthful with you. I didn't leave of my own volition. I might still be working there if I hadn't been taken. But I would like the opportunity to work at one of the best restaurants in Manhattan. I'm a good server, and I believe I could do this job."

"Kelly, the job is yours."

I stop my jaw from dropping. "Just like that?"

"The Wolfe family dines here a lot. If I can do anything to help any of their father's victims, I want to do that. I believe you can handle the job, and I would like you to have it."

"But the only reason you're giving it to me is—"

"Kelly, no. As much as I want to help Derek Wolfe's victims, I wouldn't give you the job if you didn't have any serving experience. I might try to find something else for you —in the kitchen, or upfront. But we only hire experienced servers here at The Glass House."

"All right. Thank you."

"Come with me. We'll go back to my office and get your paperwork done. When would you like to start?"

"As soon as possible, I guess."

"Perfect." Linda taps on her tablet. "How about tomorrow night? I have openings for both lunch and dinner shifts, but dinner shifts make bigger and better tips, so I'll give you the option."

I swallow. "Dinner it is then. What time do I need to be here tomorrow?"

"Dinner seatings begin at five, so get here at four and I'll have one of the experienced servers orient you. Our uniform is simple black pants and a white blouse. The pants you're wearing are fine. Do you have a white blouse?"

"Like a plain white blouse? Like what I'm wearing, only in white?"

"Absolutely. The blouse you're wearing is lovely. It just needs to be white."

"Yes, I have a white blouse."

"Excellent. You may want to buy a few more. You'll be wearing them every night, so you'll need a few if you don't want to be doing laundry every day."

I nod. "Of course. I'll do that."

"All right. Follow me to my office, and we'll get you set up."

ABOUT A HALF HOUR LATER, I'm fully employed and ready to start at the restaurant tomorrow evening. I walk back to where Leif is still sitting on the bench in the waiting area. Already people are lining up outside for lunch. Leif has his head down, and he's typing something on his phone.

I clear my throat.

He looks up and smiles when he sees me. "You were back there a long time. Can I assume that it went well?"

"Why would you make that assumption?"

He shakes his head.

God, why did I do that? Why is my first instinct always to fight? This man is not my enemy.

"For your information, it did go well. She hired me. But only because of the Wolfe family."

"What do you mean by that?"

"She asked me why I left my previous job. What else could I tell her? It wasn't my idea to leave it. I'd probably still be in Phoenix working there but for..."

Leif rises and nods. "But for being abducted and sent to the island."

I gulp. "That's right."

"It's okay. It's good that you didn't lie."

"Except that when she found out my history, she offered me the job on the spot."

"So?"

"So the only reason I got it is because of my...*checkered* past."

"And the problem is..."

"The problem is she didn't hire me on my qualifications. I was a two-bit waitress at a local diner. I'm not qualified to work here."

"The manager thought you were."

"The manager was taking pity on me."

"So what? You got the job. If she doesn't think you can handle it, prove her wrong. Be the best damned server The Glass House has ever seen."

I feel a smile emerging on my face. I'm enjoying this—this constant sparring with Leif. I tend to spar with everyone, but he fights back. I'm actually having fun. I don't normally have fun when I'm sparring because I'm always in a bad mood. Always striking out.

But with Leif?

It's different.

Oh, I'm still lashing out. But instead of feeling like crap while I'm doing it, I'm kind of laughing inside. Enjoying it.

Sure, I could tell him that Linda said she wouldn't have given me the server position if I didn't have any actual serving experience. That she may have tried to find me something else in the restaurant. But that would be too easy. It's more fun to verbally spar with him.

"What?" He holds up his hands in mock surrender. "No comeback to that?"

"What if I fail?"

"You won't. Tell yourself that you won't. You're strong,

Kelly. You can do anything you set your mind to. You've survived the worst. It's all smooth sailing from here."

"You have no idea what I've survived."

"I have a general idea."

"From who? Aspen?" I shake my head. "She doesn't have a clue what I've survived."

"Fine. I don't know. It's all between you and your therapist. I will never say that I know exactly what you've been through. Do I have a general idea? Yes, I do."

"You may have a general idea of what I went through on that island," I say. "But that's all you have. You don't know what my life has been like. You don't know what I've been through."

He reaches toward me then, touches my upper arm.

His touch burns through me. Through the fabric of my blouse, through my skin, through my flesh and muscle, straight to my core.

I step away from his caress.

And it's difficult because what I really want to do is step toward him.

But I don't get close to people. People only lead to heartache.

"I apologize," he says.

"Get over yourself. You don't need to apologize to me."

"Apparently I do."

"You don't. No one apologizes to me."

He cocks his head, rests his gaze on me. What is he thinking? He seems confused, but I could be wrong. I've never been the best at reading people.

"Very well then," he says. "No more apologies. I'm here for you, Kelly. I'm being paid very well to be here for you. So if you don't want apologies, you will get no more from me."

"Fine," I say. "I need to go shopping."

"Okay."

"You're not going to interrogate me about why?"

"Why would I do that? Why would I question everything about you? If you say you need to go shopping, I'm taking your statement at face value. Let's go shopping."

"I have to go to Macy's. To get some white blouses for work."

"Good enough. Did I ask for an explanation?"

He laughs then. He fucking laughs. Shakes his blond head and laughs. Then he holds out his hand and ushers me out the door.

And I don't know whether to be angry or turned on.

Because it dawns on me that I'm both.

Damn.

17

LEIF

I hate shopping. I hate it with a purple passion, but Kelly got a job. This is huge. Keeping busy will help her focus —give her something else to focus on besides whatever is eating at her inside.

This is good.

I just hope she understands she must be nice to her customers. If she ends up treating them the way she treats the rest of us?

Goodbye, job.

"All right. Macy's it is," I say. "You want to get some lunch first?"

She looks at her watch. "It's only eleven."

"True, but I'm always hungry."

"I think I'd rather do the shopping first, if you don't mind."

I clutch my hand to my heart. "Wait, did I hear you right? Did you just ask me if I *mind*?"

She rolls her eyes at me. "You know what? Screw that. Shopping first. You don't have to come."

"Would I miss shopping with you?" This time *I* roll my eyes. "Never in a million years." I hail a cab.

"I can't afford to be taking cabs everywhere," she says.

"Did I ask you to pay?"

A taxi stops for us, and the cabbie gets out and opens the back door for Kelly. She scrambles in, and I get in beside her.

The cabbie takes the driver's seat. "Where to, mister?"

Kelly shakes her head with a huff. "What makes you think he's in charge? Why are you asking him where to go?"

Oh, God...

"Uh...sorry." The cabbie turns back to face the road. "Where to, miss?"

"That's so sexist, just *assuming* I'm a miss."

I breathe out slowly. This could go on forever if I don't put a stop to it.

"Macy's, please," I say calmly.

"You got it."

This particular cabbie is good at dodging through traffic. So good that Kelly's knuckles go white as she clasps her hands in her lap.

Interesting that she does that a lot. Holds her hands together in her lap. If I knew more about body language, I'd probably know what that means. Whatever it signifies, at least she stays quiet.

When we arrive at Macy's, I hand the cabbie my Wolfe-issued credit card and give him a handsome tip. Then we head into the store.

"I'll take it from here," Kelly says.

"You want me to just stand around and wait for you?"

"Either that or stand around and wait for me in the middle of the women's section. Which do you prefer?"

"I suppose you have a point." I shove my hands in the pockets of my pants. "Try not to be too long. I'm starving."

"No one forced you to come along."

"You have an answer for everything, don't you?"

She doesn't reply. Just harrumphs and heads toward the escalators.

She'll probably be a while, so I walk around the first floor of Macy's, glancing here and there, until my phone buzzes in my pocket.

I grab it and raise my eyebrows. "Dad?"

"Hey, Leif. How is everything going?"

"It's going. Buck and I are on an assignment from the Wolfes."

"Buck? Isn't he supposed to be on his honeymoon?"

"Yeah, but it got postponed. There's another issue with one of the girls from the island. The Wolfes wanted Buck and me on it."

"How did I not know about this? Your mother and I were at that wedding."

"We didn't find out until the reception was almost over. Buck and Aspen had to postpone their honeymoon. Aspen of course understands, since she was one of the women on the island."

"She is lovely," Dad says. "Buck is a lucky man."

"He is."

A rumble comes through the phone as my father clears his throat. "So I have some news."

"Is it good news?"

"Depends on how you look at it, I guess."

"Wait a minute. Are you and Mom all right?"

"Oh yeah, we're fine. Scarlett and Laney are fine."

"What is it?"

Another throat clear. "Falcon Bellamy is being released."

The phone slips from my fingers and clatters onto the floor of the department store. I pick it up and place it back to my ear. "What?"

"He's getting out on parole. Good behavior. All that kind of stuff."

"Oh my God..."

The Bellamy family owns the ranch next to ours, but it's a huge operation compared to our smaller one. Falcon Bellamy and I were best friends growing up. We've known each other since we were in diapers, and we were going to join the Navy together, until...

"I figured you'd want to know." Dad's voice is grim.

"God, Dad. I never went to visit him once."

"I know you didn't. You had your reasons."

"No reasons that he'll understand."

"You went to school, enlisted. Went overseas. Then you got the job working for the Wolfes. You've been busy, Leif. Anyone would understand that."

Falcon won't.

Falcon Bellamy and I were fucking blood brothers. Still are, if you believe in that kind of shit.

We were going to be SEALS together. But then...someone was killed. No one really knows the real story. Only that Falcon took the heat for it. Is he capable of murder? What a loaded question. I've taken life myself, as part of the military. You learn to live with that. You have to.

"I can't get away, Dad," I tell him. "And even if I could, I'm not sure I want to."

"You never believed Falcon was guilty."

"Truthfully, Dad? I never *wanted* to believe Falcon was guilty. But the truth is I just don't know."

"You of all people, Leif, know that there are sometimes extenuating circumstances."

"Taking a life in battle is different," I say.

"Is it?"

My father was a military man. Marines. His father wanted him to run the ranch with him right out of high school, but he chose to serve his country first. We talked a lot about the military in our household, about the focus it requires, about the strength and determination. About the love for your country, the love of service.

We never talked about the unthinkable. But soldiers, marines, sailors, airmen—sometimes they have to take lives.

Enemy lives, for sure, but they're still lives.

"I don't know, Dad. I'm standing in Macy's. I can't have this conversation right now."

"I understand," he says. "I just wanted you to know that Falcon's getting released soon. What you do with that information is up to you."

"What are you going to do? You going to go see him?"

"I went to see him every couple of months," Dad says.

I nearly drop the phone again. "You did? Why didn't you tell me?"

"Because you were busy, Leif. You were either overseas serving your country, or you were in New York working for the Wolfe family. You had your hands full. There was nothing you could do for Falcon, but there *was* something I could do."

"What exactly did you do for him?"

"I gave him friendship. The friendship he probably wanted from you, but that he couldn't have."

"Are you saying he was angry with me?"

"Not at you. He was angry that he wasn't there with you, serving his country the way you both planned to."

"That was his own damned fault."

"Like I said, there are extenuating circumstances to every story."

"I can't—" Out of the corner of my eye, I see Kelly walking toward me, carrying two Macy's bags. "I'm sorry, Dad. I have to go."

I end the call quickly and shove the phone back in my pocket.

I am *not* in the mood to deal with Kelly Taylor right now.

"I've been looking all over for you," she says. "You were supposed to stay right at the entrance."

"Was I? Funny, I don't remember taking orders from you."

"Yeah? How long did you think it would take me to find white blouses?" She lifts one of her shopping bags, gesturing to me. "I know my size, so I grabbed six of them off the rack. Now I'm done. I've been looking for you for the last ten minutes."

"You've got to be kidding me." I run a hand over my face. "Let's get one thing straight between the two of us right now. Reid Wolfe may have hired me to make sure you're safe, but I do *not* take orders from you. I don't take orders from anyone." Not anymore, anyway.

She cocks her head and narrows her pretty eyes. "Seems you take orders from Reid Wolfe."

Fuck it all, the woman knows how to spear a knife right into my gut. "Actually, I don't. He gives me a lot of leeway in my assignments. And even if I did take orders from him, he's paying me very well. You're not paying me a damned red cent, lady."

She drops her jaw.

And I wait.

I wait for her nasty retort. Or for her sarcastic remark.

But it doesn't come.

I'll be damned.

Kelly Taylor's got nothing.

I can't help a smile. "I've finally rendered you speechless."

She huffs and walks toward the door.

I follow.

I follow because it's my job.

And because her ass looks damned nice in those black pants.

Once we're outside, I nod down the street to a café I like. "We're having lunch there."

"What if I—"

"You are welcome to get into a cab or onto the subway and go home. I am having lunch there." I turn, walk toward the café.

Once I get to the door, I look over my shoulder.

There she is, still holding her Macy's bags.

"You know," she says, "a gentlemen would've offered to carry my bags."

"Who the hell told you I was a gentleman?" I open the door to the café, wait for her to enter, laughing uproariously until we're seated.

18

KELLY

Leif and I get a table near the back of the café, and once a server comes by with waters, I open my menu to have something to do.

He seems different now. I'm not sure how, and I'm not sure I like it.

Operative words being *not sure.*

Because part of me *does* like it.

I'm not sure why.

I scan the menu and decide on a turkey and avocado sandwich on sourdough.

Except now, if I close my menu, I'll have to look at Leif, so I continue scanning, reading every entry once, twice, three times.

"Interesting reading?" he says from across the table.

I don't bother looking up. "Just deciding what I'd like to eat, if that's all right with you."

"I like this place," he says.

"Did I ask you if you like it?"

"Nope." He peeks over my menu. "What I was going to say

is that I like this place, and I always get the same thing. The Reuben sandwich. They have this delicious marble rye. And they make their thousand island dressing in-house. It's more savory than commercial thousand island."

"Again, did I ask?"

"You didn't. I don't care. That's what I'm having, and I felt like telling you."

"I hate sauerkraut," I say.

"Did I ask?" he says dryly.

I almost want to laugh. I almost want to laugh because he's giving me a taste of my own medicine. While normally I hate that, from him it almost seems...

Endearing?

No, that can't be.

"They have the best chocolate pie," Leif continues.

"I don't eat chocolate."

"Did I ask?" This time his tone is snide.

And it's not even slightly endearing. I don't joke about chocolate.

"Hello," a woman's voice says. "I'm Terry and I'll be your server today. Would you like anything to drink besides your water?"

I look up. Terry is blond and perky and can't take her eyes off of Leif.

Which, for some reason, bugs the hell out of me.

I decide to order first, if only to draw her gaze away from Leif. "Yes. I'd like a Diet Coke."

"Absolutely." She beams as she returns to my companion. "And for you, sir?"

"Bourbon. Basil Hayden's. Neat. And also a Diet Coke."

Bourbon? He's drinking during the day?

A lot of people drink at lunch. I don't drink much at all, so it seems odd to me.

"Absolutely." Terry makes a few notes. "I'll get these up for you right away. Are you ready to order, or do you need more time?"

"I know what I want." Leif looks at me. "Kelly?"

I close the menu, lamenting that now I'm going to have to talk to Leif. "I'll have the turkey and avocado on sourdough. A side salad, Italian dressing."

"And you, sir?" Perky Terry asks.

"The Reuben on marble rye. Side of fries. Extra ketchup." Leif gives her a wide grin.

Terry's cheeks redden, and she giggles. "Absolutely, sir." She turns around and walks away from the table.

I watch Leif.

Leif watches Terry.

I seethe.

"So you're a day drinker?" I ask.

"No."

"But you just—"

"I guess you bring it out in me, Kelly."

My cheeks warm.

Am I truly that difficult?

I already know the answer. Macy and I have talked about it *ad nauseum.*

Which reminds me. I have a session with Macy this afternoon.

Terry returns momentarily with our drinks, still beaming at Leif.

Which really gnaws at my insides.

Leif thanks her and then takes a drink of his bourbon, followed by a drink of Diet Coke.

"Diet Coke chaser?" I say.

"Yeah. You want to try it?"

I shake my head. "No, thank you."

So many questions I want to ask Leif. He knows so much about my life—at least those five years I was on the island—but I know absolutely nothing about his.

All I know is that he was a Navy SEAL.

But how do I talk to this man when he so obviously hates me? I can't even blame him for hating me. I'm not nice to people.

Or, as Macy says... I'm not nice to people who get too close.

I was perfectly cordial to Linda Parker at The Glass House, and I ended up with a job.

But try to get close to me? Get into my inner circle?

My claws come out.

Macy says it's because of my childhood. Because of my mother. A mother is supposed to love her child more than anyone else, but all mine did was hurt me, so I'm scared to get close to anyone else. I come out fighting instead of letting them in.

She's right, of course.

I need to try harder.

So I attempt a smile. "Why do you like a Reuben sandwich so much?"

"You're asking this time?" He raises his eyebrows, which makes him look... I don't know. "Because I do. Why do you like turkey and avocado?"

I sigh. I suppose I had that coming. I've been nothing but nasty to him for the last twenty-four hours.

So I decide to answer his question. "I've always loved turkey. I didn't get it much as a kid. My mom was always working on

Thanksgiving, but sometimes I got invited to a friend's house. They always sent me home with some turkey leftovers."

Which my mother always threw away, but I leave that part of the story out.

Leif lifts his eyebrows. "Did you truly just answer a question without being snotty or sarcastic?"

I scoff. "First time for everything, right?"

He lets out a breath. "Clearly you're back to your old self."

I open my mouth to respond when Terry brings our sandwiches, giving Leif her brightest smile. She slides the Reuben in front of him before she serves me.

"What ever happened to ladies first?" I ask, my tone laced with acid.

"God, Kelly..." Leif shakes his head.

Terry reddens. "Goodness, I'm sorry. I didn't realize you'd be offended. His plate was a little bit heavier so I set it down first."

Is she telling me the truth? I want to disbelieve her. Assume she was flirting with Leif and treating me with disdain.

But in my heart I know she wasn't. As Macy is fond of saying, "Sometimes a cigar is just a cigar." She doesn't quote Sigmund Freud a lot, but that's one of her favorites.

Leif is glaring at me as Terry turns and walks away.

"You owe her an apology," he says.

"I don't apologize."

"Maybe you should. You just hurt her feelings for no reason. She set our plates down within a microsecond of each other. And she said herself that my plate was heavier, which it is. My sandwich is twice the size of yours, and I have fries."

I open my mouth, but again, nothing comes out.

Until— "I apologize," I squeak out.

"Don't bother apologizing to me. I'm used to you. You should apologize to Terry when she returns."

He's right. I absolutely should.

I also know that I absolutely won't.

I'll just never come back here again. I'll never see Terry again.

So why do I have this nagging feeling in my gut? Will apologizing to Terry help it go away?

I'm tired of always feeling this way. I wonder if this is how drug addicts or cigarette smokers feel when they're cut off and need that next hit.

Like something pecking at the back of your neck.

Because that's what it is for me.

Something pecks at me, and it just never stops. Like an addiction.

I take a bite of my salad and then wipe the drip of dressing from my lips with my napkin.

The Italian dressing is too sweet, which drives me crazy. Why do restaurants like to put sugar in everything? Italian dressing is supposed to be savory, not sweet. I bet Buck would hate this.

Of course, the Tollhouse Café is not a tiny restaurant. It's a brewpub, and it caters to the masses.

Leif takes a big bite of his sandwich, and one strand of sauerkraut hangs out over his lower lip. He slurps it up quickly and then dabs at his lips with his napkin.

"How's your sandwich?" he asks.

"I haven't tried it yet."

If he cared, he would know that. He would've seen that I only took a bite of my salad.

Funny, after that kiss last night, I thought he was attracted to me.

I must've completely misread that. Why else would he kiss me? Because he's a man and he was horny and I was there. It's what men do.

I finish my salad, all the while lamenting over the sweetness of the dressing, and I finally take a bite of my sandwich.

Unlike the salad, the sandwich is delicious. Turkey and avocado is always an intoxicating combination for me and it's dressed with some kind of garlic aioli.

I swallow. "Delicious."

"The sandwich?" he asks.

"Yeah, you asked if I liked it. It's delicious."

He nods. "Good." Then he takes another bite of his own sandwich, which is already half gone. As are his fries.

Terry has come by to refill his Diet Coke twice.

Each time she swings by, I think about apologizing to her.

And each time, I don't.

Once we're done, Leif signals for the check, which Terry brings quickly. He gives her his credit card before she leaves, and within thirty seconds she's back.

Buck signs the receipt and stands. "Let's go."

He's clearly angry at me. Glaring, actually.

But always a gentleman—despite what he says—he allows me to go first.

When I get to the exit, I turn. "Excuse me for a moment. I need to use the restroom."

"Fine. I'll be outside."

I turn back into the restaurant, but I bypass the restroom, looking for Terry.

I find her on the way to a table to deliver an order. I don't interrupt her, but once she's done with the order, I waylay her in her path.

"Terry?"

"Yes?"

"I'd like to apologize for being rude to you. You didn't deserve that. I just had a..."

"Don't worry about it. We all have bad days." She smiles. "I enjoyed serving you and your companion."

"Leif. His name is Leif."

"How long have you two been together?"

"We're not together." The words come out automatically. They're true, after all. Except...something inside me kind of saddens.

"You're not?" Her demeanor brightens.

"No."

Terry fishes a pen out of her apron pocket. "Would you mind giving him my number then?"

Something surges into my gut. A feeling I don't like. That need to lash out.

But I came in here to apologize to this woman. She clearly deserves an apology from me. However, that doesn't mean I want to give Leif her number.

"Sure." I say.

"Really? Great." She writes her name and number on her pad, rips off the page, and hands it to me. "I appreciate that."

"Sure. No problem."

"You guys have a great rest of your day." She smiles. A big wide smile on her ridiculously pretty face.

"Thank you. You too." I leave the restaurant, shoving the piece of paper into my purse.

"Did you apologize?" Leif asks when I meet him on the sidewalk.

"Apologize? I went to the bathroom."

"Nice try. I watched you. You walked right past the bathroom."

"Maybe I went to the back."

"Did I not tell you this is one of my favorite places? I come here a lot. I know exactly where the restrooms are, and there isn't one in the back."

"Fine. So I apologized."

"Good. I'm proud of you."

I scoff. "Proud of me? Just who are *you* to be proud of me?"

"God damn. You know what? I take it back. I take it all fucking back." He stands out toward the street to hail a cab.

When a taxi slides across the lanes and stops for us, Leif doesn't wait for the cabbie. He opens the back door, and I get in. He gives the cabbie my address, and then he closes the door without getting inside the cab.

"Wait!" I yell.

But the cabbie drives off, leaving Leif standing on the sidewalk.

19

LEIF

I need a break from her.

Honestly, I don't know if she apologized to Terry. She said she did, but if she's telling the truth, her apology was probably trite and condescending. I go back into the restaurant, because Terry deserves a real apology.

I didn't do anything wrong, but I can't leave things the way they are.

I walk through the dining room, but I don't see her, so I waylay another waitress. "You know where Terry is?"

"I think she just went on break," the server says. "You can probably find her in the break room."

"Where's the break room?"

She nods toward the back. "By the restrooms."

"The restroom is in the back?"

She laughs. "Yeah. We have two sets of restrooms. You didn't know that?"

"I do now."

Damn. So Kelly *was* telling the truth. She did go to the restroom. But she also lied. She didn't apologize to Terry.

Christ...

I head toward the back, dodging the servers and customers, until I find—yes—another set of restrooms and an open doorway leading into another room with a couple couches and small tables.

Terry sits at the table, looking at her phone.

I clear my throat. "Terry?"

"Yes?" She turns and looks over her shoulder, and then she smiles broadly. "Oh, hello."

"I'm Leif," I say.

"Yes, I know. Your name was on your credit card. What can I do for you?"

"I came to apologize for my...er...companion. She's been going through some stuff. She shouldn't have treated you the way she did."

She lets out a nervous laugh. "I've been treated a lot worse by paying customers."

"Not by paying customers who accompany me," I say. "I'm sorry for her behavior."

"That's kind of you. But she already apologized."

I stop my eyebrows from flying off my forehead. "She did?"

Damn, she told me the truth, and I didn't believe her. My bad.

"Yeah, she came in right after you guys left," Terry says. "She apologized. And she told me you weren't together."

"No. We're not a couple."

"I know." Terry blushes. "I was very glad to hear that. I hope you didn't think it was too forward that I gave her my number to give to you."

Again, I stop the eyebrows. "Oh, no, not too forward at all."

"I hope you call me sometime."

"I'm only in town for a little while," I say.

"Oh." She looks down but a second later she meets my gaze with a sultry smile. "Well, maybe we could get together while you're here. I've lived here a long time. Do you need someone to show you around?"

She's not really my type. She looks too young, first of all, and she's a little flirty for my taste. But maybe I should go out with her. I'm incredibly attracted to Kelly, but she is clearly not interested. Will never be interested. And as beautiful as she is on the outside, inside she's ugly as a hag.

"How about tonight?" I ask Terry.

"That'd be great. I get off at four thirty."

"Awesome. You want me to pick you up here?"

"Sure. But I have to go home and change."

"Okay. I'll pick you up at your home then." I nod to her pad. "Write down your address for me. Put down your phone number too."

"Don't you already have that?"

"Right." I turn and glance toward the entrance. Kelly's long gone, if she even still has the number. "Yeah, but it doesn't hurt to be safe."

She smiles, scribbles on her pad, and then hands the paper to me.

"What time are you usually done cleaning up after work?"

"It doesn't take long. Could you pick me up around six?"

"I'll be there." I smile. "I'm looking forward to it."

"Me too. See you tonight."

I turn, walk back out of the restaurant.

Terry isn't a woman I'm interested in, but going out will be good for me. Maybe I'll find out I like her. You never know.

I hail a cab. When I'm back at the building, back on the fourth floor, I stop at Kelly's door and knock.

I'm being paid to see first to her safety. I want to make sure she got home okay.

So I knock.

And I knock again.

And then I panic.

Shit. I just put her in a cab. New York cabbies are notoriously honest, but still... What if I put her into the one cab that meant her harm?

And Reid Wolfe is paying me a shit ton of money to see to her safety.

I grab my wallet out of my pocket. Shoved underneath my driver's licenses is something Kelly doesn't know I have. The key card to her apartment.

Reid gave it to me in case of an emergency, and even though I'm not sure right now is an emergency, I can't take the chance. Her safety is my responsibility. The Wolfe family trusts me, and I cannot betray their trust.

Of course, entering Kelly's apartment without her permission may well be breaking *her* trust.

But right now, her safety is more important than that. It trumps everything.

I slide the key card through the reader, and the door clicks open.

I open the door, walk in stealthily.

"Kelly!" I yell.

No response.

I look around for any signs of evidence that she's here. A phone on the table. A purse hung over a chair.

But there's nothing.

Not that I know what this apartment normally looks like. This is my first time inside.

I continue to walk quietly through the small hallway and through the living area past the kitchen.

The door to her bedroom is closed.

Dare I enter?

I knock.

Again no response.

She could be asleep, so I knock a bit louder.

And again...nothing.

I turn the knob and open the door. "Kelly?"

The door to her en suite bathroom is also closed, so I walk toward it, swiftly open it and—

A bloodcurdling scream.

Coming from Kelly.

Naked Kelly.

A towel is on a puddle on the floor in front of her. Rather than clutching it to her, she must have lost her grip.

I gape.

I can't help myself.

She's a goddess.

Gorgeous round tits with light brown nipples. And those nipples? They're standing straight out.

A curvy hourglass figure, gorgeous legs that are long and shapely. Her red hair is wet and hangs in strings around her milky shoulders.

I gaze again at her legs. The scars. On her thighs. My God...

"Get the hell out of here!" she yells. "You fucking perv!"

Right. She's absolutely right.

What am I thinking? Staring at her as if I've never seen a naked woman before. I leave, closing the door.

"God, I'm so sorry," I say through the closed door. "I was worried. You didn't answer when I knocked."

No reply. Not that I expect one. She's angry and rightfully so.

And damn, I can't get the image of her naked body out of my head. I think it's seared in there permanently, as if it's branded into my brain.

I sit down on her bed to wait for her.

"Are you gone yet?" Her angry voice comes through the door.

"No. I'm waiting for you."

"Then you'll be waiting a long freaking time, because I'm not leaving this bathroom until you're out of this apartment."

"Fine. I'll wait for you in the living room."

"No. You will leave my apartment. Now. How the hell did you get in here anyway?"

A valid question, and one I will answer honestly. "Reid gave me a key in case of an emergency."

"Did he now? Leave your key on the kitchen counter. Then leave."

"I'll leave, but I won't leave my key, Kelly. It's important that I have it for emergencies."

"What's your excuse today? This is hardly an emergency."

"Yeah, it *is* an emergency. I put you in a cab, and I should've gone with you. So when I got back, I wanted to make sure you were okay. When you didn't answer your door, I was concerned, so I came in."

"You mean you broke in."

"No, I came in. I was concerned about your wellbeing. You're my responsibility—"

"Let's get this straight, Leif. I'm *no one's* responsibility. I haven't ever been anyone's responsibility other than my own.

No one has ever taken care of me, and I don't need anyone to take care of me now."

Her words strike me.

Just as I suspected, she has a backstory. Her childhood was less than great.

She's never been anyone's responsibility? Not her parents'? The state's? No one's?

Scary stuff.

I don't know what she's been through, but it was far from good.

"Kelly, I—"

"I can still hear you, so that means you're still here. Get the fuck out!"

I could win this battle. She has to come out of her bathroom at some point. But she's stubborn. So damned stubborn. She will stay in there for hours, and I have a stupid date tonight.

"Fine," I say. "But this isn't over. I will *not* be leaving my key, and you and I need to have a chat."

"I see no need for a chat," she says. "I don't want to hear your voice again."

"Fine. I'm leaving."

I leave her bedroom and shut the door behind me, and then—not leaving my key card—I let myself out of her apartment and head toward my own.

And I try to ignore the hard-on I still have from seeing her naked.

20

KELLY

"Are you still there?" I yell from behind the bathroom door.

No reply.

Of course, he could be not answering on purpose.

Pervert, staring at me like he's a starving dog and I'm a freaking turkey leg.

I have so many scars. And they're not just from the island.

But my God, he was gaping at me like I was a feast on a platter.

Fucking degenerate.

"You better not be there!" I yell.

I wrap myself in a towel and carefully open the door from the bathroom into the bedroom.

Thank God. He's not in my bedroom. He could easily still be in the apartment, but at least I can get dressed.

I hastily pull on some jeans and a T-shirt, and then I head back into the bathroom to comb out my hair. I'm not going anywhere for the rest of the day, so I let it air dry.

Linda told me I'd have to wear it up to work—either in a bun or ponytail.

Once I'm dressed, I pad out of my bedroom quietly, expecting to find Leif lurking somewhere.

But, after casing the small place, I realize he's not.

And for some reason...that irks me too.

Everything irks me.

Especially the fact that Leif Ramsey has a key to my apartment. I head back into my bedroom where my phone is charging and yank it off of the cord. Time to call Reid Wolfe.

"Wolfe Enterprises," a robotic voice says into my ear.

"This is Kelly Taylor. I need to talk to Reid Wolfe."

I'll get right through. There's a standing order at Wolfe Enterprises that any of us women from the island can get right through to whichever Wolfe we want to talk to, even if they're in a meeting.

A few seconds pass and—

"Kelly? This is Reid. What can I help you with?"

"You can change the locks on my door. Make sure Leif Ramsey does *not* have a key card."

"I'm afraid I can't do that. I'm happy to change your locks if you feel there's been a threat against you, but Leif will always have a key card."

"He broke in on me today. Barged into my bathroom and saw me naked."

Silence on the other end of the line. I get the distinct feeling that Reid Wolfe is holding back a chuckle.

"I'm sorry to hear that, Kelly, but I'm sure he had a good reason."

"He said he was concerned."

"And why was he concerned?"

"Because he knocked on my door and I didn't answer. But

did it occur to him that I might be in the bathroom? Which I was. I'd just gotten out of the shower. I didn't hear anyone knock."

"I can see how this is upsetting to you, but I trust Leif Ramsey. I trust him with my own life. With the life of my wife and daughter. And I trust him with your life."

"Isn't it more important that *I* trust him?"

Nothing for a few seconds.

I know what's going on. Reid is trying to compose himself. He won't raise his voice at me. He never raises his voice at me, even though there are times when I know he wants to.

Even though there are times when he certainly has every right to.

"I understand your concern," he finally says. "But Leif Ramsey is the best in the business. You will be safe on his watch, and as long as there are threats being made against you, I want the best keeping you safe."

"You know exactly how you can keep me safe," I say. "Get rid of Brindley."

"As I've told you countless times, Brindley denies that she sent you any messages. We have no evidence—"

"Me! I'm your evidence. I say it was her."

Silence again.

Reid's composing himself again.

Finally, "Kelly, someone is making threats to you. We've seen your texts. They've come from a burner phone, and Brindley denies sending them. We have watched her since these texts began, and we have never seen her go anywhere where she could purchase a burner phone. No burner phones have been delivered to her address."

"So she called someone. Met them somewhere. Had them deliver a burner phone to her."

"You're not hearing me. We've had her watched."

"Have you searched her place?"

He's quiet.

"Just as I thought. You haven't searched her place."

"She has a right to privacy. We will not violate that."

"For all you know, she could have a stash of burner phones in her apartment."

A heavy sigh whooshes into my ear. "We are putting your protection as our top priority. That is why Leif Ramsey is here to protect you. That is why he has a key to your place. He will not violate your trust."

"He already did. Today."

"I'll speak to him. Perhaps he jumped the gun a bit today, but his heart was in the right place. I can assure you of that."

"His heart? Or some other part of his anatomy? He saw me naked!"

"I'm sorry about that. I'm sure he apologized."

"What do you expect when you barge into a woman's bathroom?"

"As I said, I will speak to him. And as I also said, I'm sure he apologized."

I say nothing.

"Did he apologize, Kelly?"

"Yes," I say through gritted teeth. "He apologized."

"Ramsey is a good man. He probably feels terrible about this."

"He should."

"Of course he should. He didn't want to violate your privacy any more than you wanted it violated. He was just concerned, Kelly. He was doing his job."

"So you're not going to change my locks?"

"I'm happy to change your locks, Kelly. But I will give Leif a key."

"For God's sake. Maybe I should just move out of here." I scan the place. This was supposed to be my safe haven, the one place that only I had access to. Now, this untouched home is forever soiled.

"That is certainly your prerogative," Reid says. "But you won't have the kind of round-the-clock security you have at the current building. Plus, anywhere else you live, you'll have to pay rent."

"Maybe I can pay rent. For your information, I got a job today."

"That's wonderful. I'm very glad to hear that. What kind of job did you get?"

"I'll be waiting tables at The Glass House. For the dinner seating."

"The Glass House is a fine restaurant. You should do very well there. Congratulations."

"So I won't be in your hair much longer."

Another few seconds of silence.

Yep, he's composing himself.

"We don't consider you *in our hair*, Kelly. We're happy to provide for you. To try to make up, in some small way, for what our father put you through. We know we can't erase those years. But we can at least see that you are safe and getting the help that you need."

My instinct is to strike back. Strike first and strike hard.

But these people don't mean me any harm. Funny. The first people in my life who don't.

I don't know any other way than to strike first and strike hard.

Saying thank you is so hard for me, but I have done it. Once or twice.

I open my mouth, will the words to come forth. "I know it doesn't always seem like it, but I do appreciate what you do for me. For all of us."

Silence for a few seconds. No doubt he's stunned by the fact that I am actually grateful.

"I know that, Kelly," he finally says. "And you should know that wherever you go, you will always have the support of the Wolfe family should you ever need it."

"All right. Bye." I end the call.

I draw in a breath, let it out slowly.

So Leif Ramsey has a key to my place.

He can come and go as he pleases.

In my heart, even as angry as I am—and I'm always angry —I know he didn't barge into my place on purpose.

Well, maybe on purpose, but not to gawk at me naked— even though he did.

He was truly concerned.

What bothers me more than the violation of my privacy is that...

I don't hate that he saw me naked.

In fact...I kind of like it.

21

LEIF

I knock on the door to Terry's apartment, and another woman—young with brown hair and eyes and wearing...not much—answers.

"Hey, I'm looking for Terry."

"All right. You must be Leif. I'm Shauna, one of Terry's roommates. Come on in."

"*One* of Terry's roommates?"

I look around the small apartment. There's one living room, and maybe two bedrooms.

"Yeah. Five of us live here, actually."

"Five of you?"

"Yeah, we were all friends in college, and we came out here to New York to find jobs. As you probably know, it's expensive to live here."

She's not wrong, but five roommates? Man...

Good enough. I don't have to worry about her inviting me back to her place.

"Where are the rest of you?"

"Bonnie, Keisha, and Lucy are all at work. I'm off today."

"Oh? What do you do?"

"I'm a server. All five of us are. I actually work with Terry." She smiles at me. "Which is a bummer, because like I said, I'm off today. Terry told me she met you at work."

I clear my throat. "Yeah."

"I wish I'd been working." She smiles again.

"So you guys all went to college together, huh?"

"Yeah. We just graduated a year ago."

Oh, God. That means Terry is about twenty-two or twenty-three years old. Way too young for me. This date will be short.

Terry comes scrambling out of one of the doorways. She looks nice, in flared jeans and a T-shirt that shows a sliver of her belly. What is it about that tiny sliver of belly that's so damned sexy? Though the thought isn't for Terry. I'm remembering what Kelly wore the night we had lasagna with Buck and Aspen. Better yet...Kelly naked, her eyes wide, her nipples sticking out...

"Hi, Leif. I see you've met Shauna."

I compose myself and take a look around the tiny apartment. "Yes, she was telling me that five of you live here together."

"Pretty cramped, right? We all get along really well. And don't worry. I can leave a sock on the bedroom door." She lifts her eyebrows.

Oh, God...

Not the sock on the bedroom door thing.

Yeah, this'll be an early night.

Plus the fact that—as pretty as Terry is, and as nice as she looks tonight—I can't get the visual of naked Kelly out of my mind.

"Where are we going?" she asks.

"I thought we'd get some dinner."

Except...I didn't make any reservations. Damn. But there is one place I know where I can always get in.

"How does pizza sound?"

"I'm a little sensitive to gluten. I'll have to have gluten-free crust."

"I'm sorry to hear that. Do you have celiac disease?"

She shakes her head. "Oh no. I just try to stay away from it. Wheat belly and all."

Wheat belly? Is that a term I should know? I decide not to press the issue because I don't really care.

"Well...I can see if they offer gluten-free crust."

"I'm sure they do. Most places do these days."

"Good enough."

We leave her apartment building and grab a cab, and I give the cabbie the address to my favorite pizza place. It's in a more rundown area, but I can always get in.

Terry chatters in my ear during the cab ride, asking inane questions about my life, and when we finally get there, I'm glad for the reprieve. Service is quick here at Gianni's Pizza, and once we get food, I'll eat and I won't have to talk.

"Leif!" Gianni's brother, Mikey, greets me. "Haven't seen you in a while."

"I've been in California," I say, "but I'm back on a job now."

"And who is this lovely lady?"

"This is Terry. Terry, this is Mikey. He's the owner's brother."

"Your favorite table happens to be available," Mikey says. "Follow me."

My favorite table is in the back, out of the commotion. Gianni's stays busy, but they always have a table available, especially for Buck and me. Most of their business is delivery and takeout.

The table is dark and secluded, with a candle burning in the center. It screams romance, and I'm not looking for that kind of evening.

I pull Mikey aside. "Can you give me a little light tonight?"

"Sure." He glances at Terry. "You certain about that?"

"Yeah. I'm totally certain."

"Good enough."

Mikey slides two menus onto the table, and I—always a gentleman despite what I said to Kelly in anger—hold out the chair for Terry.

I take a seat, and true to Mikey's word, within a few minutes the lights are brighter over the table.

Terry looks up. "What happened?"

"I don't know. This is an old building. Wiring issues probably."

A little white lie never hurts.

I open my menu, hoping that there is a gluten-free option. If there's not, I'm going to have to find somewhere else for us to eat, and since I don't have reservations, that will be an issue.

I scan the menu. Yes! At the bottom is an asterisk with "gluten-free option available" next to it.

Thank God.

"They do have gluten-free crust," I say to Terry.

"But that does present a problem," she says, "because you don't want gluten-free crust and I do."

"That's no problem. We'll get separate pizzas."

Her eyes widen, showcasing her thick mascaraed lashes. "My goodness, I can't eat a whole pizza myself."

"Sure you can. Get a ten-inch. And if you don't eat it all, you can take it home."

She smiles at me. "You're so smart. That's a great idea."

Really. I'm smart because I suggested she get her own pizza and take the excess home.

Wait until she finds out what I know about geopolitics. I'll be a fucking genius. Not that I think that subject will come up.

A busboy comes by with glasses of water and sets them in front of us. "Your waiter will be with you soon," he says before he leaves.

"So what kind of pizza do you like?" I ask.

"Vegetarian. I don't eat meat."

"Are you vegan?"

"No. I eat cheese and eggs. Only cheese really. I don't like eggs."

"I see. They have a lot of good toppings here."

"Yeah..." She glances at her menu. "Since I'm getting my own gluten-free pizza, I think I'll get artichoke hearts, black olives, and mushrooms."

Ugh. That sounds awful. "Great. I'm getting pepperoni and sausage."

"Such a man," she gushes.

"I happen to know a lot of ladies who like pepperoni and sausage," I counter.

"Yeah, but it's kind of a man's pizza, don't you think?"

"No, not really." I look down at my menu to have something to do. "Do you want a salad?"

"Yes, I think I'll have a vegetable salad with oil and vinegar. Maybe a side of garlic bread."

"That's a lot of food."

"But you said I could take it home."

"True, I did. And you can."

I hope she doesn't think I'm being cheap. Then again, it doesn't matter, because I really don't care.

All I want is for this date to be over.

BECAUSE I'M A GENTLEMAN, I see Terry to the door of her apartment, and I carry her takeout container.

"I had a lovely time," she says. "Thank you so much."

"Yeah, it was fun." I hand her the box holding her leftover pizza. "Good night."

She smiles coyly. "Don't you want to come in?"

I feign a yawn. "I can't. Early day tomorrow."

"Oh." She looks down at the ground for a moment.

I have no intention of seeing her again, but I don't like hurting a woman's feelings. I'm hoping she won't push it.

"Anyway, good night," I say again.

"Can we go out again?" she asks.

"I'll call you," I say.

"Okay. I look forward to hearing from you."

But the tone of her voice says it all. She won't be hearing from me, and she knows that.

I take her key from her, unlock the door, and give her a kiss on the cheek. "Good night."

She nods simply and closes the door behind her.

I don't like hurting a woman's feelings. I shouldn't have asked Terry out to begin with. Rather, I shouldn't have accepted when she asked me. I've never gotten used to women asking men out. I'm kind of an old school Texan. I knew Terry and I weren't right for each other, and I had a feeling she was too young for me—which turned out to be very true. She talked a lot about bands I've never heard of and how she and four roommates have pajama parties and pillow fights. Not my scene for sure.

I grab a cab back to the Wolfe building and head up to my apartment.

But then I drop my jaw.

"What the hell are you doing out here?"

22

KELLY

"You have me at a disadvantage," I say. "I don't have a key to just let myself in to *your* apartment."

He rolls his eyes at me. "I apologized for that, Kelly. I told you why I did it. I was concerned."

"Maybe I've been concerned about you. Where have *you* been tonight?"

He walks to his door, unlocks it, holds it open for me to enter. "It's not really any of your business where I was tonight."

"Why not? It seems to be your business where *I* am every second."

"Did you come here to argue? Because you know as well as I do that it is my *job* to know where you are. To see to your safety."

"Even if it means barging into my bathroom."

"I can apologize again, but I don't think it will do any good." He shakes his head. "To say that I regret it would be an understatement, but I have my reasons for barging in."

"Yeah. To peek at me. What are you? Some kind of peeping Tom?"

"Oh my God." He rakes his fingers through his blond hair and looks up toward the ceiling. "What the hell did I do in my godforsaken life to deserve any of this?"

"I ask myself that on the daily," I mutter.

"What?" he asks, his tone exasperated.

"Never mind."

"What can I do for you, Kelly?"

"I just want to know where you were."

"Do you? Fine. I'll tell you. I was on a date. With our waitress from this afternoon. Terry. And by the way, I think you were supposed to give me her number?"

My cheeks warm.

How the hell does he know about that?

"You see, Kelly, the reason I put you in a cab and stayed after lunch today is because I wanted to apologize to Terry. I was going to apologize for your behavior, even though I personally had nothing to apologize for. So I went in, and I—"

"Then you found out I wasn't lying, didn't you? I *did* apologize to her."

"Yes."

"So now you owe *me* an apology," I say.

"I don't owe you shit."

"You owed me an apology for barging in on me."

"Yes, I *did* owe you an apology for that. And I apologized. That's done."

"And you also owe me an apology for not believing that I apologized to Terry."

"You'll be waiting a long time for that one. Now, why the hell are you here?"

"I told you. I wanted to know where you were."

"You know. I was out on a date with Terry. Now I'm home."

"She's too young for you," I say.

"Not that it's any of your business, but I agree. I won't be seeing her again."

"So it doesn't matter that I didn't give you her number, then."

"Actually, it does matter. She asked you to give it to me, and you said you would. But you didn't. Why?"

"I just told you. She's too young for you."

"She's over twenty-one. Maybe I like younger women?"

"You just said you didn't. That you agree."

"But you had no way of knowing that when you didn't give me her number, did you?"

He's right, of course. No matter how much I fight. No matter how much I strike first and strike hard, I always know, in my own mind, when I'm not being fair. It happens a lot lately, and this is certainly one of those times.

I have no claim on Leif Ramsey. Why would he want me anyway? I've been nothing but a bitch to him since we were introduced.

"If that's all, Kelly," Leif says, "I'm exhausted, and I'd like to go to bed."

I set my hands on my hips. "It's not all, actually."

"Fine. What the hell do you want?"

"I want you to..."

"What? I'm ageing here."

"I want you to come and have a look at my apartment. To make sure everything is secure."

He rakes his fingers through his blond hair again. "Fine. Come on."

He follows me out of his place, and next door to mine, where I slide the card through the reader and open it. He allows me to go in first, and he follows.

"So what's the problem? What don't you think might be secure?"

"Could you just have a look around the perimeters? Make sure that everything's okay?"

"Of course, but do you have any reason to believe that it's not? Did you get another text?"

I could lie. I could tell him that I got another text. Then he would demand to see my phone, and I wouldn't be able to produce a text.

"No. It's just that, after you barged in this afternoon, I've been a little concerned."

"There's no need to be concerned. I had a key. No one else can get in here."

"If it's all the same to you, I'd like you to check things out."

"Absolutely. Glad to do it."

His tone doesn't indicate that he's glad at all, and I want to call him out on it.

But I zip my lips shut.

I'm so wildly attracted to him, and that scares me more than anything.

Leif walks around the apartment, searches every corner, picks up the landline telephone, takes the back of the receiver off, and then checks the main unit. He looks under every lamp, rolls back the carpet sitting under the coffee table. He even goes to my bookshelf and looks inside all of my books.

I don't know what could be hiding in a book, but he's the expert.

Once he's cased the living room, he moves into the

kitchen, opens my refrigerator, looks through all the produce and other items. He doesn't check the freezer though.

Then he walks to the door of my bedroom and looks at me. "May I enter?"

"Yeah."

It was nice that he asked. He didn't have to, and if he hadn't, I probably would've said something.

He is a nice guy, and I've been treating him like complete crap.

He enters the bedroom and begins a thorough search as he did in the living room. He looks under the bed, between the mattress and box springs. Underneath all the lamps. And again he takes apart the phone units sitting on my nightstand. He looks through all my dresser drawers, and I open my mouth to say something, but then I close it.

I asked for this.

He's just being thorough.

Still...he's going through my bras and panties.

My skin heats.

But he's done with the top drawer soon, and he goes to the next drawer, which houses my socks.

Next are T-shirts, and below that, what I call a junk drawer.

Then he goes into the closet—a walk-in closet, so there's a lot of ground to cover. And he covers it. Again, he's very thorough, checking through all my garments that are hanging. Would someone really stick a bug in clothes?

But where he's *really* thorough—as if I didn't think he were thorough before—is with my shoes.

He looks at every single one, and he plays with the heels.

"What exactly are you doing?" I can't help asking.

"You asked me to check things out. Shoes are a great place to hide a bug."

"They are?"

"Yeah. No one ever thinks to look there, except for people like me."

I have several pairs of shoes, so his task takes some time. When he finally puts the last one down—

"Only the bathroom now."

My flesh heats again. The bathroom. Where he saw me naked.

Where my body burst into flames at his gaze.

He looks at me, cocking his head. Is he waiting for permission?

"Okay." I shrug. "The bathroom."

He walks to the door—a little more slowly—draws in a breath, and opens it.

The first place he looks is inside the medicine cabinet behind the mirror above the sink. Great. Now he'll see my birth control pills and my anxiety meds.

What the hell? This was my idea, not his.

He moves all the bottles of medication, opening them and looking inside. Then he looks behind the cabinet itself, attempting to pull it off the wall, but he's unsuccessful.

"If you have a screwdriver, I can check behind here and make sure there's nothing, but I doubt there is. Depends on how thorough you want me to be."

"Sorry. I don't have a screwdriver."

"No worries."

He takes the lid off the toilet tank next, peers inside. Then he removes the toilet seat and takes a good look inside the toilet as well.

Then the cupboard below the sink, and lastly, the shower.

Once he's done, he turns to me. "This place is clean, Kelly. Nothing to worry about."

"Are you sure?"

"You just saw me look. There's nothing. No hidden cameras, no bugs, nothing. You're secure here, Kelly. I assure you."

Which means he's going to leave.

I don't want him to leave.

I want him to...

Damn. I don't know what I want. I just know I don't want to be alone. Which is strange in itself, because I've never minded being alone. When you spend half your life locked in a closet, you get used to it.

I bite my lower lip. "Thank you for doing this. Can I get you a drink or something? To repay you?"

"No, you don't need to repay me. I'm already paid. This is my job."

"Fine."

I'm feeling indignant, of course. Nothing new there.

"If that's all, then." He heads toward the door.

But I grab his arm, and I tingle at the warmth of it.

He looks over his shoulder. "Yes?"

"Don't go. Please."

23

LEIF

Please? Did that word truly just come out of Kelly Taylor's mouth?

I study her.

I look hard. I desperately try to see something beyond her physical beauty and her fight-or-flight attitude.

Is she attractive?

God, yes. She's the most beautiful woman I've seen in a long time. I've always liked redheads, and though her hair is a little darker, she still qualifies. She's wearing blue leggings and a large white T-shirt. Hardly the stuff of wet dreams, but she makes it look like it came straight out of Victoria's Secret.

My dick responds to her, which I'm not happy about. She's my charge. I'm supposed to protect her, not fuck her.

But although I find her physically attractive, her personality? Not so much.

"What do you want?" I ask her.

"I'm just...scared. I'm so tired of being scared."

"I understand. I've been scared myself."

She scoffs. "When were you ever scared?"

Really? Did she just go there? "I was a Navy SEAL, Kelly. My life was in peril on the daily when I was overseas. I lost friends over there. Buck and I came back, but four of our friends didn't."

She swallows. I don't hear anything but I see her throat move.

Good. That got to her. It's about time she realizes that she's not the only person who's ever been through bad stuff. She's not the only person who's ever been to hell and back. I feel for her. I do. I feel for every one of those women who was violated on that godforsaken island. But the other ones that I know? Katelyn? Aspen? Jenna? Carly?

They're all healing. They're taking a proactive attitude.

Kelly? There's nothing proactive about her. She's all reactive, pure and simple, and she reacts by striking.

"So...good night." I head back toward the door.

But again she grabs my arm. And damn... Her touch. My cock is already hard.

She's a beautiful woman, for sure, but I don't like her.

Still... It's been a while for me, and I am a man, after all.

"Can I tell you?" she asks.

I breathe in, let out slowly. "Tell me what?"

"What it was like."

"On the island?" I shake my head. "I can't hear that, Kelly. My imagination is bad enough. I hate what was done to you women. And I understand more than you know."

I expect a sarcastic or smart-ass comment to come from her, so I'm surprised as hell when—

"Tell me about the war."

"I wasn't in the middle of a war," I remind her.

"I suppose not. Where were you?"

"Afghanistan. A couple tours."

"And Buck was with you?"

"He was."

"You came back and he came back," she says. "Who didn't?"

"You really want to know?"

"I do. I think I really do."

"Okay."

I unbutton my shirt.

She gasps. "Now wait a minute."

"Don't get the wrong idea," I say. "If I wanted something more from you, I'd have tried it before now. But this is the best way for me to explain to you who I lost over there."

I continue unbuttoning, and her cheeks turn red. Will she like what she sees? Most women do. But I'm not unbuttoning my shirt for her to ogle me.

I slide the shirt off of my shoulders and hang it over the chair standing by the door.

Then I turn around so she can see my back.

She gasps. A huge and audible gasp.

"That symbol in the middle is the Navy SEAL Trident. You already know they call me Phoenix, right?"

"Yes."

"See the Phoenix? The bird erupting in flames? That's me. And the Buck? The deer with his antlers on fire? That's Buck."

She says nothing. I imagine she's nodding, but I don't turn to look.

"The rest of those images are my friends. You'll notice that they all have halos. Ghost, Wolf, Ace, and Eagle."

I jerk when her warm finger touches my flesh. But I don't move. I let her. I relish her touch as she traces the outline of the phoenix, of the buck, of all the other images and their halos.

I'm not sure how many minutes I stand there, how many minutes she touches me, but the warmth from her finger travels straight through me, all the way to my core.

All the way to my cock.

Finally—

"I had no idea," she says.

I turn to face her, meet her gaze. "We don't go over there for our health. We go over to serve our country, and it's not always pretty. More often than not, it's downright ugly."

"It's beautiful work," she says. "The tattoo, I mean. What you did over there..."

"Wasn't beautiful, for sure. Buck and I had them done when we got back. He has the same tattoo." I hold up my wrist, showing the SEAL trident again. "Plus this one."

"The Navy SEAL logo again," she says.

"It's so much more than a logo."

She nods, but she doesn't ask me to elaborate.

Good, because I'm not sure I can. I can tell her the meaning of the symbol, but I can't tell her the feelings it invokes in me.

You have to be a SEAL to understand.

Her gaze is focused on my chest now—

"I have a tattoo," she says.

"Do you?"

"I do. Would you like to see it?"

"Sure."

She unbuttons her blouse, and a pink lace bra becomes visible, but she stops unbuttoning when it's loose enough to pull over her shoulder.

She turns around, and on her left shoulder is a volleyball, surrounded by wilted black roses.

I can't help widening my eyes. "That's nice work, but it's something I'd expect to see on Aspen, not you."

She turns back, a frown on her face. "What? You think Aspen is the only woman in the world who plays volleyball?"

"No. I just didn't know *you* did."

"I don't. But I did when I was a kid. I was good too, until —" She shuts her mouth abruptly.

"Until what?"

"Nothing. I don't know why I showed you. I don't go around showing people my tattoo. I just thought...since you showed me yours..."

"I showed you mine because you asked about my friends."

"Yeah. Well, my tattoo doesn't have anything to do with friends."

"There are some people out there who just like ink," I say. "But those who have only one or two tattoos usually have them for a specific reason. I was just wondering what yours was."

"It's a reminder," she says.

"A reminder of what?"

"A reminder that no matter how happy I get—how happy I allow myself to get—it will all eventually be taken away."

Does that explain the black wilted roses? Her words sink into my heart. My God, what she's been through... I can't help myself. I reach toward Kelly and I trail a finger over her porcelain cheek.

"I'm so sorry," I say.

She steps away from my touch. "For what?"

"For whatever happened to you on that island—or

anywhere else—that made you feel like you don't deserve to be happy."

She crosses her arms. "I don't need your pity."

"You don't have my pity," I say. "Just my concern."

"Are you kidding me? The pity coming from you is so thick I could cut it with a knife."

"It's not pity, Kelly. It's empathy. Pure and simple. I don't know your story, but I know my own. I know what it feels like to think life will never be good again."

"Oh you do?" Her tone is sardonic.

I shake my head. "No one has your story. It's your own and unique to you. But other people do have stories, some not as bad as yours...and some worse."

"You think you have a story worse than mine?"

"No," I say truthfully, absently reaching to touch her. I stop just shy of her cheekbone. "I don't."

Because I think her story transcends her time on that island. I think there's much more to Kelly Taylor than any of us know.

24

KELLY

Without thinking, I launch myself at him.

I grab him, pull his head down, force his lips onto mine.

And I kiss him.

I kiss him for a few seconds, and I'm not sure he's going to respond until—

He parts his lips and sweeps his tongue into my mouth.

This isn't our first kiss. We both know what to expect.

Angry passion.

Leif Ramsey is the perfect outlet for my angry passion.

I stalk forward, pushing him up against the wall next to my door, and I force him to deepen the kiss.

Until—

He breaks away, turns me around quickly until my back is against the wall, and his blue eyes stare into me.

"Don't," he growls. "Don't do this unless you're willing to go all the way."

"Just kiss me. Kiss me again," I grit out.

"I'll kiss you, Kelly. I want to kiss you. I want to do a lot more than kiss you, and I think you know that. So this is your get-out-of-jail-free card. Tell me to leave now, and I will."

I open my mouth.

I open my mouth to yell at him. Tell him to get out. Tell him I'm not ready for this, which I'm not.

But all that comes out is—

"Don't leave."

He looks down at me, cups my cheek. His touch singes me.

"You sure? Are you totally fucking sure? Because if I kiss you again, we both know what's going to happen."

"I'm sure."

He takes both my cheeks in his hands—holds my face—and grips my gaze for what seems like an eternity.

Just when I'm about ready to yell at him to kiss me—

"I'm not. I'm not sure at all." He lets me go and steps toward the door.

"Don't go," I say. "Please. I need this."

"You don't need this," he says. "And I am not a *this* for someone to need. I take my job protecting you seriously, Kelly, and we both know I won't be doing my job if I allow this to happen."

I drop my gaze to his jeans. His bulge is apparent. My God, he must be huge.

And for the first time in—ever?—I want that part of a man inside me. I feel empty and aching.

"Leif..."

He raises his eyebrows. "Is that the first time you've called me by my name? No. It's the second."

"Is it? I... I don't know."

"That's just it. You don't know. You don't know *me*. And I don't know you. We have a pretty good idea of what each other's lives have been like up until now, but that isn't enough."

"You're telling me you've never gone to bed with a woman without knowing who she is?" I scoff.

"I'm not saying that at all. What I *am* saying is that you're under my protection, and if I allow this to happen, I won't be doing my job."

He's right, of course. I understand what his job is. I know I'm a mess. I know how I feel on the inside, and it's not always how I project myself on the outside. I strike first. I strike hard. To avoid being hurt myself.

When in reality?

I'm aching. Aching on the inside and on the outside for something more. For a friend. For a companion.

For a lover.

And Leif Ramsey, damn him, is so fucking gorgeous. I don't even like blond men, but he looks like he walked off a Viking ship.

I nod, then. Bite my lower lip. "I understand."

I expect him to leave then, so when he steps toward me and cups my cheek again, I drop my jaw.

"Am I finally seeing the real Kelly?"

I close my mouth. Is he? Am I allowing him to see what's on the inside?

"Sometimes I'm not sure who the real Kelly is," I say.

"I don't believe that for a minute." He trails his finger from my cheek over my still bare shoulder. "I think the real Kelly isn't the harsh woman you like to portray to others. I think somewhere underneath that hard exterior is someone who's soft and gentle. Or at least was once."

Is he correct?

Was I *ever* soft and gentle?

I suppose I was. I suppose I wanted to be. I still want to be. I'm just afraid that if I let my guard down, I'll get hurt again.

Because I always get hurt.

"So tell me," he says. "Am I right?"

"You don't know what it's been like," I say.

"Right. I don't. Only *you* know your own story, Kelly. If you want to talk, I'm happy to listen."

"I would like to talk."

"You can talk to Macy. Or Aspen. Or to Zee. I know either of them would be happy to talk with you."

"What if I want to talk to you?"

"I'm here. For whatever you need."

"Whatever I need?"

He nods.

"I need you to kiss me again."

He steps backward then, rakes his fingers through his thick blond hair. "I'm not made of steel, you know. You know how beautiful you are, Kelly. Why do you insist on teasing me like this?"

"I'm not teasing you."

"Hell, yeah, you are. You know I can't go to bed with you. My job is to protect you, not to get involved with you sexually. Yet you insist on..." He shakes his head. "Good night."

This time he does leave.

He opens the door and closes it behind him.

I go to the door and slink down against it, until I'm sitting, my back against the hard door.

I'm throbbing all over, and my flesh is hot, and then cold, and then hot again.

My lips still sting from his kiss, and my cheek burns from his touch.

And that volleyball surrounded by roses on my shoulder?
It's burning into my skin, like a brand.
And I remember.
I remember why it's there.

I CRY myself to sleep that night. My birthday. My tenth birthday.

My mother destroyed my volleyball—the only thing I ever bought with my own money. I scraped together pennies and nickels, dug out the money buried underneath the couch cushions, saved money on the rare occasion that my mother gave me a few coins. And sometimes, when my mother wasn't home, I went to the neighboring houses, asked if I could do any chores for money.

More often than not, I was told no, but an elderly couple who lived a few houses down took pity on me and always let me come in and vacuum or dust for a dollar or two.

I'll buy another volleyball.

But I'll hide it. Because if my mother finds that, she'll destroy it like she did the first.

And then...

I will get out of this house as soon as I can.

ONCE I TURNED EIGHTEEN, my mother kicked me out anyway. She actually helped me with that last promise.

By the time my eleventh birthday rolled around, I had enough money to buy a new volleyball, which I stored at one of my friends' houses.

My mother never knew I had it.

Still, that didn't keep her from making my life miserable.

By the time I was fourteen, she didn't lock me in the closet anymore. She didn't hit me anymore. I was as big as she was at that point, and because of all the volleyball and other sports I played at school and afterwards, I was more muscular than she was.

Many times I dreamed of pounding her into a pulp.

But I didn't.

Part of her still had power over me. The power of motherhood. I wanted her love so badly that I allowed her the power long after I should have ended it.

I'll never forgive her for that.

I don't even know if she's still alive.

And I don't care.

Funny. All the rest of the women from the island had people to call—people who were thrilled to find out they were still alive rather than dead as they all thought.

But not me.

I had no one.

Which is why I'm stuck here, living in the housing provided by the Wolfes. With Leif Ramsey as my personal bodyguard.

I rise then.

And I open the door.

25

LEIF

Sitting in an empty hallway, my back to Kelly's front door, isn't where I should be.

It took all the strength and willpower I possess to leave that apartment. I can't believe how much I want her. Yearn for her. This woman—this woman who has been through so much—who fights against everything and everyone who tries to get close to her.

I can't imagine the pain she's suffered.

But I can't be the one to add to it.

And taking her into my bed? Making love to her? It would feel good for both of us. But the pleasure would be solely physical, and she would regret it afterward.

Would I regret it?

Making love to a beautiful woman?

Hell, no.

But it's not really in my job description.

I suppress a laugh. The Wolfes sent Buck after Aspen, and he ended up sleeping with her.

In fact, they fell in love, and I swear to God, after all

they've both been through, they are two of the happiest people in the universe. Does anything make sense anymore?

Time to go to bed.

Because God knows what Kelly Taylor will have in mind for me tomorrow.

I moved to rise when—

The door opens, and Kelly stands there.

"Oh! What are you still doing here?"

"Just leaving," I say as I stand.

"Don't."

"We've been through this, Kelly."

"I know. You're right. But I'm not in the mood to be right tonight."

God damn her. If she only knew what she was doing to me.

I sigh, take in her sheer beauty. "God, you're beautiful."

Her lips turn up into a smile.

An actual smile.

I can't help but let out a soft scoff. "Wow. I wasn't sure you could do that."

Her lips draw back into a frown.

Then I realize with a laugh that I'm acting exactly like she acts. I'm lashing out for no reason.

"I apologize," I say.

"You don't have to apologize. I get why you said that."

"Do you? Are you so unhappy that you've forgotten how to smile?"

"I think I just smiled. At least you said I did. It's hard for me to tell anymore."

I reach a finger out, trace her lower lip. "You have beautiful lips. You should smile more often. You're a beautiful woman, Kelly. Every part of you is beautiful."

"Except what comes out of my mouth?" she says haughtily.

"Yeah. When you're right, you're right."

She moves to close the door, but I stick my foot inside it. "Maybe we should talk."

"I don't want to talk, Leif. I didn't open this door to come find you to talk."

"Yeah. I know."

"You want me as much as I want you."

I start to smile but stop myself. "You think so?"

"Do you kiss every woman like that?"

"As a matter fact, I do. I like to kiss."

She's right though. Kissing Kelly was special. Spectacular, even. There was a rawness, an ache, a need. Something I haven't felt in a long time, if ever.

I've only been in love once, and it was with a woman from home. Falcon Bellamy's sister Robin.

Damn.

That was so long ago. The last couple times I've been home to visit my folks, I haven't even seen her. Robin is too sweet and innocent for someone like me now. I've seen things no one should have to see, had experiences that no one should have to experience.

But...

So has the woman before me. Kelly is far from too sweet and innocent for me. We have more things in common than not. I don't know her whole story, but she doesn't know mine either.

Yet we seem to fit together. The physical chemistry between us is hot.

And damn...

It's been a long time since I've wanted a woman like this.

And as much as I thought I was in love with Robin Bellamy all those years ago, I don't ever remember feeling this much of an ache for her.

I reenter Kelly's apartment, and I look her straight in her beautiful blue eyes.

"This isn't a game, Kelly. I told you before. If you want me to stop, you need to tell me now. Because once we start, I may not be able to."

"You stopped before."

"I did. And it was one of the hardest things I've ever done."

Her lips quirk up into that pretty smile again.

"There you go. There's that smile."

This time she doesn't frown. She keeps the smile on her face. "No one has ever told me they like my smile."

"You're kidding me."

"No one's ever told me I'm beautiful either."

I drop my jaw. "I'm sure you had tons of boyfriends, you know... Before..."

"Before the island?" She shakes her head. "I worked my ass off, living paycheck to paycheck, trying to make ends meet. I didn't have time to date."

"Surely you were asked out."

"A few times. By customers. Other employees at the restaurant. But I never returned their interest."

"But you're returning mine?"

"Yeah, and damned if I know why." Then she looks me over. My shirt is still unbuttoned. "Well, I guess I know why."

I resist the big grin that wants to spread across my face. Sure, I'm attractive to women. I've known that since I got through puberty.

"I think you're gorgeous," I say, "but I'm not interested in a one-time thing, especially not with you."

"Why not?"

"You know why. You're my job."

"I'm a human being, Leif. I'm not a job."

I lift my eyebrows. "You're right. I apologize."

She drops her jaw. "I said something that makes sense to you?"

"Absolutely. You're a human being. First and foremost, you're a unique individual. I'm glad you know that."

"Macy helped me with that. And the therapists at the retreat center. They were good. Really good."

"Were they?" I can't help a chuckle.

"I know why you're asking me that. I know how I've treated you, and I'm going to tell you right now that my instinct is to lash out at you."

"I'm not surprised."

"They've told me..."

"Go ahead."

"No. It's just too private to talk about. Can't we just...go to bed?"

"We could, but isn't that the *most* private thing we could do together?"

"Not really." She scoffs.

Facepalm. Literally a palm to my face. What the hell was I thinking? "I'm sorry. I shouldn't have said that."

"It *should* be private. A private thing between adults. Both parties should consent. But those five years on the island did a number on me. I don't think of it as a private thing anymore."

"It's a miracle that you want it at all," I say.

"Not really. Macy said my desires would come back. She

said I'd probably be surprised when they did, and that they might come sooner rather than later."

"And *are* you surprised?"

"Yeah. Although looking at you, who wouldn't want you?"

This time I don't resist. I let the grin spread across my face, splitting it. "You can be sweet when you want to be."

"Sweet? Never."

"Maybe I should be the judge of that." I pull her toward me, tip her chin, and kiss her lips.

She opens for me, and I swipe my tongue in between her lips. I kiss her, hard and passionately, and she returns the kiss with equal sentiment.

It's not our first kiss, but it's a kiss like the first time you ever kiss someone. It's *that* exciting. Even a touch of taboo about it.

I deepen the kiss, kicking her door shut with my foot.

I don't know if we'll make it into the bedroom, but if we do? I won't stop this time.

This time, I'm all in.

26

KELLY

Within a few minutes, I'm not just being kissed. I'm being devoured.

And to have this happen to me—to my body, with my consent, with my complete desire and yearning—is something.

Something amazing.

I don't think I've ever wanted a man the way I want Leif, and though it doesn't make any sense—other than the fact that he's incredibly good-looking—I'm ready to go with it. I'm ready to let him explore me, do whatever he wants to me.

I know. I know that if I tell him to stop, he will stop.

He makes all that big-man talk about "tell me now if you want to stop, because I won't be able to." But this man? This Ex-Navy SEAL? He will stop if I ask him to stop.

I brush the shirt back over his shoulders until it lands on my hardwood floor. Then I touch him. I run my hands down his neck, over his broad shoulders, savoring the hardness and the warmth of them.

I touch his chest, his hard pecs. He's so blond he has almost no chest hair, and what little he has is nearly white.

He's perfect. His nipples look like light copper coins, and when I run my fingertips over them, they harden for me.

Then there's the bulge. The bulge I already noticed in his jeans. He must be huge, and I want huge. If I have huge, it will burn through me, erase everything that's been done down there before—without my consent.

It will be perfect.

We continue to kiss as he discards my blouse. My bra is pink lace. I'm not really a pink-lace person, and I'm not sure why I bought this bra. I wore it today for good luck on my job interview.

He groans and cups my breasts through my bra.

Then he breaks the kiss. "God, you're so fucking beautiful."

I simply sigh. I'm determined not to lash out. I want to enjoy this. Once it's over, he'll probably quit his job, and I may never see him again.

I have to be okay with that.

He reaches around my back and deftly unclasps my bra, pulling it off of me. My breasts fall against my chest, and my nipples are already hard.

"You have a pretty blush on top of your breasts," he says. "So beautiful." He cups them again, thumbs my nipples, making me jolt.

My God.

To have a man touch me—not in violence but in gentleness.

Except I'm not sure I want gentleness from Leif Ramsey either.

I want to be taken. Taken and pillaged, burned through to expunge all the horrible things that have been done to my body.

I don't have a lot of scars like some of the other girls. Just a few on my back and on my inner thighs.

But I can't think about them now. Leif probably has scars too, although I don't see any on his chest or back. Then again, that tattoo takes up his entire back. Perhaps it's more than a memorial to his fallen friends. Perhaps it's covering something else.

He leads me over to the couch, sits down beside me, lowers his head, and flicks his tongue over one nipple.

A spark travels through me, ricocheting and landing between my legs.

God, between my legs. I still have feeling there, after all this time.

He flicks the nipple and then he closes his lips around it and sucks while he fingers the other one, twisting it lightly.

Oh my God. So good. Feels so freaking good.

Leif Ramsey knows his way around a woman's body, and I want him to really enjoy mine.

He slides his hand—the one that was fondling my nipple—down my belly to my pants, unbuttoning them and then unzipping them.

He stops for a moment.

Does he think I'm going to tell him to stop?

I don't want to talk, for fear that I'll lash out when I don't mean to. I simply cover my hand with his and push it underneath the waistband of my bikini panties.

He groans against my breast, sucks the nipple harder, and then takes over, moving his hand over my vulva and between my legs.

Another groan, and he drops the nipple. "You're wet."

"Am I?"

He looks at me then, burns me with his gaze. "You want this as much as I do."

"I thought that was obvious."

"Nothing's obvious with you, Kelly." Then he smashes his mouth to mine, kisses me deeply, hungrily.

He toys with my wet folds, and all I want is to get out of these clothes. For him to get out of his clothes, to thrash naked on the couch, on my bed, on the floor. On the kitchen table. I don't care.

I wriggle my hips, trying to shimmy out of my pants. All I succeed in doing is kicking off my shoes.

I don't want to break the kiss, but I do, and I gasp in a breath.

"Please," I pant out. "Clothes. I want to take off my clothes."

He lifts an eyebrow. "All right. Please do."

Is he expecting a striptease? He's in for a surprise. I get rid of my clothes in an instant, nothing sexy about it. Just crumpled pants and panties on the floor along with my shoes.

I'm sitting naked on the couch, and all I can think about is his lips. Those lips that are so firm on mine, and how they might feel on my inner thighs, between my legs, sucking on my pussy.

"You sure about this, Kelly?"

"Oh, for God's sake, already," I huff out. "I'm sure. I'm wet. I'm ready. I'm sure."

"If you say so."

Leif rises, kicks off his shoes, removes his jeans, his underwear, his socks.

I look away for a moment, and I'm not sure why.

Until he says, "Look at me. Look at me, Kelly."

I turn and stare at him. He's standing above me as I sit on the couch. His dick springs out from a blond bush, and just as I suspected...

He's huge.

He's huge enough to corrode through me and obliterate everything that's ever happened to my body.

And that's what I need.

That's what I'm yearning for.

I gape at him. I can't help myself.

"You okay?" he asks.

"Yes. I'm okay. Please stop asking. I want this. I promise you if I change my mind at any moment, I will let you know."

"Good enough." He grabs his jeans, fishes something out of the pocket.

It's a condom, and I expect him to rip it open, sheath himself, and get into me quickly.

But he doesn't. He simply sets it on the coffee table, and then he kneels before me, spreads my legs.

"You have a beautiful pussy, Kelly. You're so wet and glistening."

I heat all over. From embarrassment? From arousal?

I'm not sure, and I don't even care.

All I know is his lips are pink and swollen from all the kissing we've done, and I can't wait to feel them between my legs.

He scoots me toward him so my pussy is mere inches from his mouth. Then he smiles at me. He looks at me from between my legs, and he smiles at me.

But the scars...

Surely he must notice them.

The thought flees from my mind.

He's so handsome, and that smile could melt the hardest heart.

I'm sure mine is one of the hardest out there.

I'm not quite ready to melt my heart yet, but I *am* ready for him to suck my pussy.

He touches me first. Smooths his fingers over the scars on my thighs. I wait for him to say something, ready to strike back.

But he doesn't. He simply caresses me, sliding his fingers from my thighs to the folds of my pussy and then—

His lips are on me, his tongue sliding up and down my folds, swirling around my clit.

My God... The feelings that roll through me are so much more intense than I imagined. I imagined something purely physical. But I'm feeling...

I'm feeling...

I don't know.

I can't put any of it into words, and I don't want to. Words might somehow bastardize it. I want to just go with it, enjoy the feelings. Let them flow through me and around me and over me and under me.

And maybe erase some of the shit from my life.

He groans against my flesh, licking and sucking, and every time his tongue touches my clit, I grasp cushions of the couch, my knuckles white. It's just right out of reach. That feeling—that intense, emotional—

And then—

Something shatters within me, and the world crowns in my body, like an explosion.

Except it's not an explosion. It's more of an implosion. Everything pulsing toward my core—that place between my legs where he's sucking, eating.

Growling, lapping at my inner thighs.

"That's it," he groans. "Come for me. Come all over my face."

I've never felt anything like this. I've had orgasms before, or so I thought.

But this...

My thoughts give way to my feelings, and I sink. I sink into the couch. Into a sea of happiness and contentment that I never knew existed.

I relax, relax around me. And I think...

I think maybe...

Maybe I'll be okay.

Leif slides his fingers into me, adding to the sensation, and I find myself right on the brink again...

So I let go.

I close my eyes, sink farther into the couch, and I let everything go.

Somehow I'm on my back now, my eyes still closed, when—

"Open your eyes, Kelly. Open your eyes and look at me."

My eyes pop open, and there is Leif—his handsome face, his full lips, his searing blue eyes—hovering over me, his dick between my legs.

"You ready?" he asks.

"God, yes."

He thrusts into me.

Even though I'm wet and sated from orgasms, he burns through me like his cock is on fire. Such a good burn. A fast burn.

And with that fire, he burns away all the horrid things that happened to me down there. He gives my body back to me.

And I let out a moan. A long slow moan.

"Leif..."

"God, baby, you are so fucking tight."

He pulls out and pushes back in, and I feel the burn again. I relish the burn. I fucking love the burn.

In, out, in, out...

Slowly at first, and then he increases his speed, grunting over me, and I close my eyes—

"No. Those eyes, Kelly. They stay open. Watch me. Watch me fuck you."

Again my eyes pop open, as if in obedience to his command.

I'm not an obedient type of girl, but damn...

So I watch. I watch him fuck me. I watch his eyes, and then I look between our bodies, watch his cock plunge in and out of me.

And again... The beauty of our joining erases all the negativity from that part of my body.

That's why I wanted this. That's why I *need* this.

"I want you to come again," he growls. "Touch your clit if you have to, Kelly. Come again."

But I don't have to touch my clit. His pubic bone is doing that for me every time he thrusts inside me. And I'm on my way. I'm on my way—

"Yes!" I shout, as I implode once again, all my blood boiling through my veins and rushing straight to my pussy.

"Yeah, that's it. You're so hot, baby. God, I'm going to come. Going to come—" He grits his teeth. "Fuck, Kelly!"

He thrusts inside me so far that I'm not sure where he ends and I begin.

All I know is I can feel every pulse of his dick as I'm

reeling from my own orgasm, and I feel burned. Heated. Scarred.

Scarred in a good way.

He burned all the evil from me. Everything that happened on that island is now gone.

And I'm new.

My body is new.

27

LEIF

Damn.

Chalk it up to another exercise of bad judgment, but I can't bring myself to be sorry. She's freaking amazing. Being inside Kelly was...surreal.

I move off of her, as the couch is pretty narrow, and quickly dispose of the condom. When I return, she's still lying with her eyes shut.

"Kelly?"

"Hmm?"

"Let me get you into bed."

I sweep her into my arms and carry her into her bedroom, where I lay her down on her bed. I cover her, and then I return to the living room and get my clothes on.

Then I check on her again. Her eyes are closed, and a soft snore escapes her throat.

"Kelly?"

No response.

I don't want to leave her, but I don't want to stay either. I could leave a note. Let her know I'm in my apartment if she needs me.

Strangely, I have an urge to climb in bed next to her and sleep beside her tonight.

But I can't let that happen. I already let enough happen.

I GENTLY NUDGE her on the shoulder. "Kelly?"

Nothing.

I nudge her harder. "Kelly."

This time she sleepily opens her eyes. "Hi."

"Hi." I smile. "I'm going to go now, okay?"

"No. Please stay."

Damn. Those are fighting words. She has no idea how much I want to stay, to sleep next to her, but as attracted as I am to her physically...

I can't even finish the thought.

"I think it's best if I go back to my own place."

She harrumphs and turns away from me. "Fine then."

"I'll check in with you first thing tomorrow."

"I start my new job tomorrow," she mutters, still not looking at me.

"Right. I know. But you said that's not until the evening shift."

"No. But I'm fine."

"Okay. I accept that. I'm still checking in on you tomorrow." I kiss her ear. "Good night, Kelly."

I leave her bedroom, close her door so that it's slightly cracked.

I'm not sure I should leave. I've left her vulnerable, and maybe I should spend the night here at this place.

I lie down on the couch, wishing I could crawl into bed next to her and settle in. I pull a throw blanket over myself.

Nothing like a good climax inside a beautiful woman to relax me enough to get to sleep very quickly—even on a narrow couch.

~

"WAKE UP!"

I jerk my eyes open.

Kelly stands above me. As I wipe the blur out of my eyes, I see that she's still naked.

Damn.

"What are you still doing here?" she demands. "I thought you said you were leaving."

A yawn splits my face. "I... I didn't want to leave you alone."

"You've told me before how safe I am here."

"You are safe here. But we..."

"Fucked. We *fucked*, Leif."

"Yeah. I guess we did."

"You guess?"

"For God's sake, Kelly, can you give me a minute to wake up?" I sit up on the couch, get my bearings. I hate sleeping in my clothes. It's so uncomfortable. Normally I sleep in my underwear.

"You got any coffee?" I ask.

She grabs a pillow from a chair and attempts to cover herself. "I'm sure there's plenty of coffee over at your place."

"Then...do you have a robe?" I say angrily.

"This is my place. If I want to walk around naked, I will."

I rake my fingers through my hair, which I'm sure is a mass of unruly blond waves. "What's with the pillow then?"

I have no idea what else to say to her. She was so sweet last night, and she responded to me so completely when we made love. Now?

Old Kelly is back.

I don't know why I expected anything different.

In fact, I *didn't* expect anything different.

I stand, stretch my arms over my head. Then I amble into her kitchen.

"What do you think you're doing?" she demands.

"I'm going to make a pot of coffee, if that's all right with you."

As a matter of fact, that's not all right with me.

I expect those words any minute.

But oddly, they don't come. I find the coffee maker, root around for the grounds, and start a pot. Then I open the refrigerator.

Again, I expect a sarcastic and nasty comment, but I don't get one.

She is such an enigma to me, even though I understand her in a lot of ways. Her troubles didn't begin on that island. She's made that clear.

I wish I could secretly look at her therapy files. I want to know all about her. Maybe she's a new project for me.

Except I don't feel like she's a project. I feel like she's a woman I want to get to know. A woman I have intense physical chemistry with for sure, but there's so much more beneath her exterior, and I want to know everything about her. Every single thing.

I want her to know every single thing about me.

God, this is so fucked up.

Kelly arrives back in the kitchen, this time wearing a robe, thank God. My dick would never go back to normal size with her walking around naked.

She pulls two mugs out of the cupboard and sets them on the counter.

I guess that's her invitation for me to stay for coffee. "Do you have any eggs or anything? I can make some breakfast."

She doesn't answer, but she walks to the fridge and pulls out eggs, a package of bacon, and a loaf of bread.

Bacon, eggs, toast. Sounds good to me.

"Where's your frying pan?"

Again she doesn't answer, but she opens the cupboard below the oven and pulls out a frying pan. Next, she lays strips of bacon in it, places it on the stove, and turns on the burner.

Okay. I guess she's making breakfast.

The coffee is ready, and I fill each of our mugs. "Cream and sugar?" I ask.

Again she doesn't respond, so I leave her coffee on the counter, and I take mine out to the living room and sit back down on the couch.

Now what? I guess I wait for her to tell me breakfast is ready.

Why doesn't she want to talk to me?

My phone is about dead, but I check some emails and texts, reply to a few, and then my phone rings. It's Buck.

"Hey," I say.

"Hey, Phoenix. Where are you?"

"I'm at Kelly's place. Why?"

"Because I've been knocking at your door for a few minutes, and I was wondering where you were."

"What do you need?"

"Reid's been trying to get hold of you."

"Yeah, I know. I just responded to his text, but he hasn't called me."

"He got a message early this morning," Buck says, "from Kelly's mother."

I raise my eyebrows. "Oh?"

"Yeah, which is really weird, because Kelly's mother lives in Phoenix, which is three hours' time difference. And that means the text came in at like four thirty in the morning her time."

"Unless..."

"Right," Buck says. "Unless she's here in Manhattan. Or at least somewhere in this time zone."

"Can't he figure out where the text came from?"

"It came from a cell phone with the Phoenix area code. At any rate, the text said that she wants to see Kelly."

"I think that's up to Kelly, isn't it?"

"Absolutely. But I wanted to let you know, so you could bring it up to her."

"If she wants to see Kelly, why doesn't she just call her?"

"Apparently Kelly hasn't given her any of her information. Not her new address, her new cell phone number, nothing. She hasn't even seen her mother."

I stay silent a moment.

Kelly mentioned that her whole life has been difficult, and I'd bet her mother had a lot to do with that. In which case I can't blame her for not wanting to see the woman.

"Okay. I'll talk to her. I'll call Reid as soon as I have her response."

I end the call, and I walk into the kitchen where Kelly is finishing up the bacon, laying the strips on a paper towel.

"Kelly," I say.

She doesn't reply.

"You're going to have to talk to me at some point."

No reply.

"Okay. Last night was amazing. I enjoyed it immensely, and I'm pretty sure you did too. But we're going to have to table that for the moment because we have something else to deal with."

She still doesn't look my way.

"Your mother got in touch with Reid. She wants to see you."

Kelly drops the egg she was holding onto the floor, and it cracks open, its yellow yolk spilling out. I grab some paper towels and lean down to clean it up.

Once it's cleaned up and in the trash, I find Kelly in the living room seated on the couch and staring into space.

"You don't have to see her if you don't want to," I say. "I'm just relaying the message. She got in touch with Reid."

"I don't want to see her," Kelly says.

"That's fine, baby. You don't have to."

She widens her eyes at my use of *baby*.

"If I had wanted to see my mother, I would've contacted her."

"I understand. No one is going to make you do anything you don't want to do."

"Damn right. I am so *sick* of doing things I don't want to do."

"I understand."

I understand more than she knows.

"Do you want to talk about anything?" I ask.

She shakes her head.

"Okay. I'm here for you, Kelly. You can talk to me. You want me to call Macy for you?"

"I think I'm capable of calling my therapist myself if I need to."

"Yes, I was just trying to help."

"I don't need your help."

God.

"I'm going to go fix the eggs. You sit here. I'll bring you a plate of breakfast when it's done."

She stays there, still silent.

I amble back into the kitchen, mix up a batch of scrambled eggs, and fry them in the bacon fat. Not real heart healthy, but they're delicious that way. I throw some slices of bread in her toaster, and once they pop out I add butter. I look inside the refrigerator for jelly, but she doesn't have any. Good enough. I prefer plain butter on my toast anyway.

I fill two plates with scrambled eggs, bacon, and toast, and I take them back out to Kelly, where she's still seated on the couch. I hand her a plate of breakfast, and I'm a little surprised when she takes it.

"What do you want me to tell Reid? That you just don't want to see your mom?"

She nods and bites the top off a strip of bacon.

We eat breakfast in silence. Once we're done, I carry our plates into the kitchen, rinse them, and put them in her dishwasher.

"I have to go now," I tell her. "Would you like me to come by anytime later today?"

"No. I'm fine."

"Okay. I'm here if you need anything. What time do you have to report to work tonight?"

"Is that any of your business?"

"Only if you want it to be." I sigh, shaking my head.

Then I leave.

28

KELLY

"I got a job," I tell Macy during therapy later that morning.

"That's great, Kelly. What will you be doing?"

"Waiting tables at The Glass House."

Macy widens her eyes. "The Glass House? Really? That's one of the best restaurants in all of Manhattan."

"So I hear."

"That's amazing. You'll do well there."

"I'm a good server, for sure. But I got the job because... Well, you know."

"Because of the Wolfes?"

"Because I'm one of the island's victims. I mean, the manager asked me where I'd been working for the last five years, and what else could I say? Anything else—a lie—would have made me look bad."

"I agree. It's best to be honest. Especially with a potential employer. And if she gave you the job because of that? Then show her that you earned the job on your own."

"That's what Leif says."

"Leif?"

"Oh, yeah. I haven't seen you in a few days. Reid decided I need my own security detail because of the texts."

"I have to admit, Kelly, I agree with him."

"It's only Brindley," I say.

"We've talked about this before. Brindley denies sending you texts."

I scoff. "Why does no one believe me? She's had it out for me ever since she came to the island."

"That's just not true. It was every woman for herself on that island. You know that as well as anyone."

"It's just..."

"What?"

I shake my head. I don't know what to say. I've spent my life blaming others for my own misfortune, but maybe Brindley hasn't done anything.

"You really believe Brindley's not behind it?"

"I do. I think, Kelly, that you wanted to find someone to blame, and for some reason, you chose her. I think I may know why."

"Oh? Please enlighten me."

"You have a tendency to envy others. I think that stems from your childhood with your mother, as we've discussed. Your envy for Brindley didn't happen on the island. It happened once you were rescued."

"I see what you're getting at. Because she was only there for a couple of months."

"Exactly. She had it a lot easier than you and the rest of the women."

I don't say anything. Macy is always so on-target with me. Back at the retreat center on the island, I learned not to get so defensive with the therapists. I learned to listen to them.

Really listen and dissect what they were saying as it concerned my life. And I understand.

I haven't been able to stop getting defensive with others, but I'm certainly better at it with my therapists.

"You're probably right."

"Your childhood was something no one should have to live through. Your mother was a tyrant, and I've already told you how I think she probably suffered from borderline personality disorder. It's a disorder that can be managed, but your mother never got any help. She was also probably bipolar, which again is a disorder that can be managed with medication and therapy, but she didn't get any help. It's why you felt you were always walking on eggshells around her. You didn't know if she was going to be in one of her good moods or one of her bad moods."

"Or in one of her bad moods that was masquerading as a good mood," I say, "like when she deflated my volleyball on my birthday."

"Yes. That's such a sad story, Kelly, and it has affected your entire life."

"I know. I was always so envious of the other children, the children who had mothers and fathers who loved them. Who didn't send them to a closet and lock them in."

"Exactly. You still struggle with envy today. But it's time to move forward. Put that kind of envy behind you. You're going to have a good life now, Kelly. Everyone is in your corner. The Wolfes—"

"I haven't been treating the Wolfes very nicely."

"I know. You're going to have to make an effort there."

"But their father—"

"The Wolfe siblings are not responsible for their father's sins. You know that. They feel absolutely terrible about what their father put you women through, which is why they've tried so hard to help you."

"I know. And I am grateful."

"Have you told them that?"

"No. I haven't. It's just very hard for me to express gratitude. I haven't had that much to be grateful for in my life."

"Have you been journaling like I suggested?"

Macy is a big believer in journaling. I hate writing, so I have no choice but to shake my head. "It's just not my thing."

"True, it's not everyone's thing. Let me suggest something else. I want you to start a gratitude journal. You don't have to write your feelings down or write paragraphs and paragraphs of anything. All you need to do is every night before you go to bed, write down two things that you're thankful for that day."

"All right. That doesn't sound too bad."

"It doesn't have to be anything huge. Maybe you had a sandwich at a deli that was particularly good. You're thankful for that. It can be something that simple."

"All right." The turkey sandwich I had at the Tollhouse Café with Leif pops into my head. The salad was too sweet, but the sandwich was delicious.

Of course...that's where he met Terry...

Macy hands me a pad of paper. It's one of the yellow pads that she writes notes on. "You don't even need any special journal. Use this."

"This is a plain yellow legal pad."

"Yes, it is. A gratitude journal doesn't require any special tool, Kelly. Just paper and a pen or pencil. This will do just fine, and this way, you don't have to go out and buy a notebook or journal or anything. Just keep this notepad by your bedside, and every night, before you turn off your light, write down the day's date and two things that you're grateful for.

Maybe it's something that happened that day. A good sandwich, like I suggested. Or maybe it's something more important."

"I don't have a lot of gratitude about my life."

"I know you don't, but you should. You're alive, Kelly. You're young, you're beautiful, and you're smart. You have a new job. You have people looking out for you. You have so much going for you."

Sometimes, when Macy talks to me like this, I actually believe her. I actually believe that I'm lucky to be alive.

I certainly don't want to be dead. I do want to live. I've never thought about ending my life, not even on the island.

In fact, for me, the island wasn't all that bad. I've told Macy that, and it makes her so sad. For her to know that my childhood was so awful that being abused and tortured and violated by depraved men while in captivity on an island wasn't so bad for me.

Sure, they hurt me sometimes. They hurt me physically more than my mother ever did, but there's one thing my mother *did* do for me. She made me numb. Immune to pain after a while. So it was easy for me to compartmentalize what happened to me. To accept my fate, and to know that it would eventually be over. One of them was actually nice to me. If "nice" includes violating me with a body part rather than a knife. I called him The Dark One, though he said his name was Mr. Smith.

A lot of them used the named Smith.

I was The Dark One's favorite. For a while, anyway.

"So," Macy says, "bring your gratitude journal with you next time so I can see it. It will help me help you."

"Sure. It won't be too personal."

"Even if it is personal, I hope you'll share with me.

Knowing how you're thinking and feeling is the best way for me to help you. What else is going on? You have a new job."

"Like I said"—I sigh—"I have this new bodyguard."

"And..."

"I don't need a bodyguard."

"Kelly, you've been worried about the texts."

"I guess I just thought it was Brindley."

"What if it isn't Brindley? We need to be concerned about whoever is threatening you."

"They brought in this Navy SEAL."

"Right. Reid works with a couple of ex-SEALs."

"Yeah."

"Is he bothering you?"

"No, not really."

"Then what's the problem?"

"The problem is..."

"Yes?"

"I slept with him, Macy. I slept with Leif Ramsey."

29

LEIF

Buck and I meet with Reid in his office during lunch. He and Rock brought a spread of Thai food into the conference room, and I've got to say, I'm starving. The bacon and eggs with Kelly this morning were good, but I worked up quite an appetite last night.

Aspen and Buck are seated next to me on one side of the table, with Rock and Reid at each end. Rock's wife Lacey also joins us.

"Did you tell Kelly that her mother has requested to see her?" Reid asks me.

"Yeah, but she doesn't want to, and I don't think we should force her."

"We don't force these women to do anything," Reid says. "But this is her mother."

"I agree with Leif," Rock interjects. "You and I have no love lost for our mother."

"Our mother is a raving bitch," Reid says.

"I don't know Kelly's mother," I say, "but I get the feeling that her childhood was less than great. Sure, Kelly was abused and tortured on that island"—I wince at the thought —"but she all but told me the rest of her life wasn't a whole lot better."

"She did?" Reid asks.

"Yeah."

"I don't mean to seem surprised"—Reid furrows his brow —"but she made it pretty darn clear she didn't really want you anywhere near her."

"We've had some talks. I took her out yesterday morning to look for jobs, and she got one. She's going to be waiting tables at The Glass House. She starts tonight."

"That's great," Aspen says. "We'll have to go have dinner and give her some business, Buck."

"I don't know, baby," Buck says. "She'll probably think we're checking up on her."

Aspen nods. "Good point. I wasn't thinking. Kelly seems to take everything the wrong way."

"But it is nice to show that we're supporting her," Lacey says from across the table.

"She's funny." I shake my head. "I think, deep down, she wants support. She needs support. But something inside her just can't accept it. Which is why I don't want her to have to see her mother if she doesn't want to. I think that woman did a huge number on her."

"Only Macy would know," Reid says. "And those records are private."

"I know," I say. "If she's even truthful with Macy."

"Actually, I'm getting very good reports from Macy," Reid says. "She doesn't divulge any details, of course, but she would let us know if Kelly needed more help."

Aspen nods. "Macy is a great therapist. She helped me a lot, and I know Katelyn adores her."

"The other women like her as well," Reid agrees, "and although Kelly hasn't said anything, Macy feels they have very good rapport. She believes Kelly is making progress. So I think the sessions with Macy need to continue. For as long as Kelly wants them."

"Yes, of course," Lacey says. "But in the meantime, why can't we all support her?"

"She won't see it that way," I say. "She'll see it as us checking up on her if we go to The Glass House during her shift."

"Which is a damned shame," Rock says, "because I love that place."

"Yeah, Zee and I do too. In fact, Zee went into labor at The Glass House."

The others continue conversing, but I begin thinking...

Kelly's mother...

"Hey," I say, "do we know anything about Kelly's mother? What she's doing now?"

"Her name is Racine Taylor," Reid says.

"Have you had your investigators look into her?"

"We haven't really seen a need to," he says. "But I can certainly do that."

"You know what?" I rise. "I'll do it myself. I'm a pretty good PI."

"You're the best," Reid agrees. "But I want you concentrating on Kelly."

"She'll be working now, dinner shift at the restaurant. That will give me time to take a look into her mother."

"If you want to," Reid says. "I'll give you all the information I have. I'll email it to you."

"Good. Thanks."

"I can help with that," Buck says.

"Thanks, bro. I'll let you know if I need you."

"She's actually here in town," Reid says. "I just found out. Apparently she flew in a couple days ago."

"Even better," I say. "That way I don't have to fly to Phoenix and leave Kelly to fend for herself."

"So you're planning to see her?" Buck asks.

"Hell, yeah. One conversation with her and I should be able to figure out why Kelly is so dead set against seeing her."

Reid taps on his computer. "I just emailed you the file we have on Racine Taylor. It's not a whole lot, as we didn't see any reason to look into her any further."

"You didn't? Even when Kelly didn't want to see her mother after she got off the island?"

"A lot of the girls didn't want to see anyone right at first," Reid says. "It seemed natural. They felt humiliated, embarrassed."

"There's no reason for them to be embarrassed," Lacey says.

"No, there isn't," Aspen agrees, "but having been in their shoes, I understand. The whole situation made me feel very...weak. I'm a strong woman. An athlete. And I probably fought harder than any other woman on that island, but still, they got me in the end. It *is* humiliating. It's embarrassing. Even once you're out of it, and even once you go through all of the therapy and learn that it wasn't your fault and that they're no longer coming after you—you're still a little embarrassed."

"Are you still embarrassed, baby?" Buck asks.

"Not usually," she says. "But what happened on that island is a part of all of us now, and sometimes it creeps back in. It's normal. Ask any therapist."

"Kelly's having a more difficult time than some of the

others," I say. "And I get the feeling that her mother is behind it."

"You don't mean..." Buck says. "Behind her abduction?"

"I wasn't even thinking that." My flesh goes cold, as if my blood were freezing in my veins. "What if she was? Katelyn's cousin was behind her abduction. Aspen's teammates were behind hers. Why couldn't it be someone as close as a parent?"

"Wow..." Lacey says.

"It's just a theory," I say. "It's doubtful. But I honestly don't know much about the relationship between Kelly and her mother. All I know is that Kelly was a waitress at a diner in Phoenix for five years before she was taken. She probably wasn't living with her mother at that time."

"See what you can find out," Reid says. "My curiosity is definitely piqued. In the meantime, we won't push Kelly to see her mother."

"We shouldn't be pushing these women to do anything," Lacey says.

"Of course not," Reid agrees. "That's not what I meant."

Lacey smiles. "I know that."

"So what else is going on?" Buck asks.

"A few things. Lily's moving out of the building, which is good. She's going home to Montana. A few more women have bypassed the apartment altogether. They're leaving straight from the retreat center and going home. So right now, after Lily leaves, Francine, Marianne, Brindley, and Kelly will be the only ones in the apartment. Most of the women are now ready to be on their own or at the apartment, so if no one else comes to the apartment, we'll begin getting it ready for leasing."

"While Kelly and the others are still there?"

"It's all preliminary," Reid says. "We won't open up the apartment to anyone else until they're all ready to leave."

"Good."

Kelly won't be comfortable with anyone else living in that apartment building other than women from the island.

"Wonderful news about Lily," Aspen says. "I'll have to have lunch with her before she leaves."

"She's done very well," Lacey says. "We're all proud of her."

"It seems like all the women have done well," I say. "Except, of course for…"

"Our retreat center is top-notch," Rock says. "Riley and Matt, her husband, have brought in the best psychiatrists and psychologists that our money can buy. Most of the women are ready to leave within a year. Some of them want to go straight home. Most of them, actually. We only have two more women at the retreat center now, and we're getting great reports from their doctors."

"That's wonderful," Aspen says. "Now, what do we do with Kelly?"

They all stare at me.

"Don't look at me. I'm no therapist."

"No one says you are," Rock says. "But keep us apprised with what you find out about her mom."

"Absolutely. I absolutely will. I'll get started on that tonight. In fact, I will pay her a visit while Kelly is safe at The Glass House."

30

KELLY

For the umpteenth time, I paste a smile on my face.

"Good evening, my name is Kelly, and I'll be taking care of you this evening. May I start you off with a cocktail?"

I take the drink orders quickly for my table of six, and then I head to the bar.

I've been here for three hours, and things are going well so far. I'm a good server. I'm good at keeping a lot of things in my head at once. I'm determined to show Linda that she did the right thing by hiring me.

But Linda's not here tonight. The manager on duty is Lois, who doesn't know me from Adam.

And she's watching me like a hawk.

Hence, the pasted smile.

But I need to learn to smile. If I'm going to be waiting tables, a smile goes a long way. I learned that back at the diner. Smiling was hard for me then as well.

It's even harder for me now.

But it does get easier each time.

Macy said it would, and she hasn't steered me wrong yet.

During my break, I replay the conversation we had about Leif Ramsey.

~

"I SLEPT WITH HIM, Macy. I slept with Leif Ramsey."

Macy's eyes widen, which doesn't surprise me.

"And he's your bodyguard?"

"Something like that."

"He shouldn't have taken advantage of you like that."

My instinct is to agree with her. To say Leif took advantage of me, that I regret it.

But that's a lie. He did everything he could not to take advantage of me. Hell, I offered up the advantage on a silver platter. And I'm not a liar. I'm a lot of things, but I'm not a liar.

Strike hard and strike first has always been my motto, but something about this time with Leif makes me think differently.

"It would be easy to tell you that he took advantage of me, but he didn't. I was a willing participant, Macy."

"I see. And this is the first time since the island?"

"It was, and I almost felt like it was kind of a cleansing ritual, if that makes sense."

She nods. "It does. And you feel cleansed now?"

I think for a moment. Do I? I certainly did at the time. I felt like he was burning all the evil out of me.

And now? I have no regrets, but I know I wasn't really cleansed.

"Yes and no," I finally reply.

"Can you explain what you mean by that?"

"Sort of. Yes, meaning that I felt things—rather, my body felt things—I'm not sure I've ever felt before."

"Even before the island?"

"Yes."

"I see. And what do you mean when you say no?"

"No means that I can be objective about it. I know there's no such thing as a cleansing ritual. I know I'm the same person—with the same experiences—that I was before Leif and I had sex."

Macy smiles. "You know, I get reports from the Wolfes."

"I'm sure you do."

"You're so calm and collected during our sessions, Kelly, and your records from the retreat center at the island indicate the same thing, with the exception of when you first got there. But the reports I get from the Wolfes are vastly different."

I say nothing in reply.

She clears her throat and continues. "They say you're difficult to deal with. Sometimes downright belligerent. That you fight them on everything."

I nod. Does she expect me to deny it? Like I said, I'm not a liar.

"Can you tell me why that is?"

"I wish I could tell you," I say.

"Do you think they want something from you?"

"I... I'm not sure. I don't think you want anything from me."

"Which is why you're nice to me." She makes some notes. "The only thing I want is to help you. I understand, at the retreat center, it was difficult for you to accept that help from your doctors and therapists for the first month or so, but you came around."

I nod again.

"So why," she asks, "do you think it's so difficult to be kind to these others?"

"I don't know. I know they didn't have anything to do with what happened to me. It was their father, not them."

"Very true, but I can see how you still maybe blame them. Even subconsciously."

"It's not even them, really. You know about my childhood. You know what my mother was like. Whenever someone is kind to me, it always seems like a façade, you know? Like my mother. She would be kind to me, but in an instant, the kindness was replaced with meanness. Punishment. Abuse."

"The Wolfes aren't going to abuse you."

"I know that. Still... It's easier to keep them at arm's length."

"You didn't keep Leif Ramsey at arm's length." She smiles.

And I don't know what to say. Fortunately, our time is up.

I WON'T BE SEEING my mother. Macy understands that, but will the Wolfes? It doesn't matter. I'm too busy to think about it.

I head to my next table, take the dinner orders, and then grab the drinks from the previous table and distribute them, again with a smile on my face.

"Would you like to order any appetizers?"

"No," one of them says. "I think we're ready to order dinner."

Great. Smaller tip. Still, the smile never wavers. "Wonderful, let me tell you about the specials this evening."

I prattle off what I've memorized, take their orders, and get the order to the kitchen.

Then I do my rounds at the rest of my tables.

I stay on top of things all night, and I'm pretty darn proud of myself. I've never worked at a fine restaurant before, but so far so good. I've gotten adequate tips, about twenty percent average, but I'd like to see that go up to twenty-five. At a place like this, people can afford it. But this is my first night, so I'm satisfied.

Lois waylays me on my way back from the kitchen. "Kelly, could I have a moment?"

"Of course."

I'd like to get back to my tables, but when your new boss asks for a moment, you give it to her. I follow her to the hallway where the breakroom is.

"I just want to tell you that I think you're doing a very good job tonight."

"Oh, thank you." I hold back a sigh of relief. "I was afraid you were going say something else."

"No, not at all. I'm thrilled you're here, and I want you to know that if you ever need anything, anything at all, please feel free to come to me."

"Why would I need anything?"

"I'm not saying you will. But the Wolfe family is a huge patron of this restaurant, so anything we can do... You know."

Anger curls up my spine. I want to smack her around now. But I keep the smile pasted on. "That's very kind of you. Thank you. I should get back to my tables."

"Yes, of course. Don't let me keep you."

I'm tense now, so I head to the employees' restroom. I look in the mirror, and for a moment, I see the scared little girl locked in her closet.

I cannot be the scared little girl.

I need to be the self-assured waitress.

So I close my eyes, and I do what Macy told me to do. Visualize. Visualize someone who is capable and professional.

I open my eyes.

And there she is. Kelly Taylor, server at The Glass House. I wash my hands quickly, dry them, and head back out to see to my tables.

31

LEIF

Racine Taylor is staying at the Waldorf-Astoria.

Interesting.

I called to ask if I could see her, and she told me to meet her at the hotel bar. So here I am, waiting.

She's late.

Fifteen minutes so far, and just when I wonder if she's going to show up at all, in walks a woman who makes every head turn.

Her hair is flaming red, and her eyes are blue. She's dressed in tight black pants and a leopard-print blouse.

She's Kelly's mother all right. Her features aren't as fine as her daughter's, but there's a definite resemblance.

I rise, hold up my hand, and wave to her from the small table where I'm seated. She comes toward me, seeming to relish all the eyes on her.

I hold out my hand. "Racine Taylor?"

"Yes, I am. And you must be Leif Ramsey."

"Guilty on that charge. Please, have a seat." I hold out the chair for her.

"Aren't you the gentleman," she says.

"I try to be." I take a sip of my drink. "Are you hungry?"

"Goodness, no. I don't eat bar food."

Interesting to know. "A drink then?"

"I will never pass up a drink."

I signal to our server.

She comes quickly. "Can I get you another, sir?"

"I'm good for now, thank you, but I think the lady would like to order a drink."

"Of course. What can I get you?"

"Champagne cocktail please," Racine says.

"Coming right up."

I smile at the server and then turn back to Racine. "It's nice to meet you. As I told you on the phone, I work for the Wolfe family."

"Yes. I assume you're here to talk about my daughter, Kelly."

"I am. I was wondering if you could tell me why you want to see her."

She widens her heavily made-up eyes. "Because I'm her mother."

I take another sip of my bourbon and then clear my throat. "Kelly doesn't want to see you, Ms. Taylor."

She smiles. "Please, it's Racine." Then her smile fades into...something unreadable. "Why wouldn't she want to see me?"

"I don't know. I don't know her very well. I was hoping maybe you could shed some light on that question."

"It's absolutely terrible what happened to my daughter." She sniffles, though her eyes don't glisten with any tears. "She needs her mother now. More than ever."

"She's had the best care," I say. "A year at a retreat center, and now she's living in housing provided by the Wolfe family while she continues her therapy."

"She doesn't need therapy. She just needs her mother."

"I see. Why don't you and I have a talk, and maybe I'll be able to convince her to see you?"

"I'm not sure what there is for us to talk about. I'm her mother." She narrows her gaze. "Do you have children, Mr. Ramsey?"

"Please call me Leif, and no, I don't have any children."

She eyes my left hand. "Married?"

"No."

She smiles. "Now that is decidedly good news."

Oh my God. Is this woman going to hit on me? Kelly is twenty-eight years old, so this woman must be at least forty-eight, maybe older. She's not unattractive—I mean, she's Kelly's mother—but she has a kind of hardness about her that I can't quite place.

"Is it?" I ask.

Maybe I can get some information out of her if I let her think she has a shot.

"I'd say it is." She winks. "Wouldn't you?"

I smile. "I think it could be."

The server arrives with Racine's champagne cocktail, and she holds up her glass.

"To a memorable evening," she says.

"To a memorable evening it is." I clink my glass to hers. I believe this *will* be a memorable evening, although not for the reason she's hoping.

"Can you tell me a little bit about Kelly?" I ask.

"I'm sure you know way more than I do. I haven't seen her since... Well, you know." She chokes up. Or attempts to.

"I only met her a few days ago. The Wolfes asked me to focus solely on her security, to protect her."

"Protect her? Isn't that what *they're* doing?"

"There've been some threats against her," I say.

Racine gasps. "No! Who would threaten my child?"

"She thinks it's one of the other women from the island, but we don't agree."

"Who do *you* think it is?"

"We don't know. Whoever it is has used text messages from burner phones that can't be traced."

"If Kelly thinks it's this woman from the island, she's probably right. Kelly is a very good judge of character."

"Is she?"

"Yes, definitely. She has been since she was a child. If my daughter didn't like someone, I took it seriously."

Interesting. Does Racine have any idea how her daughter feels about *her*?

But I feel like I'm getting somewhere.

"Would you like to go somewhere a little more private?" I ask.

She takes another sip of her champagne cocktail. "What are you suggesting?"

"Dinner? In your room?"

She sets her drink down harshly. "My goodness. I'm not the kind of woman who—"

I place my hand over hers. "I'm not suggesting that at all, Racine. However, it's kind of noisy here in the bar, and I'm not sure if it will be any quieter in one of the restaurants."

"Goodness, we couldn't get into the restaurants anyway. Not without a reservation."

"Room service then. My treat."

Her shock at my outrageous suggestion dissipates. "In my room? All right."

I take another sip of my drink. "Good. I'm looking forward to it."

~

RACINE'S ROOM turns out to be a suite. What the hell does this woman do for a living? Or maybe the Wolfes are putting her up. I should've asked.

I glance at the room-service menu and decide on the New York strip. I hand it to Racine. "Whatever you'd like. I'll see that you're reimbursed."

"Please, don't worry a thing about it." She scans the menu. "I'm going to start with the Beluga caviar. And then a house salad, and the rack of lamb. What are you having?"

"The New York strip, rare."

"Excellent." She picks up the receiver on the phone. "I'd like to order some room service, please." She rattles off our selections and adds a bottle of champagne. Dom Perignon, no less.

"There, should be here in about half an hour."

Great. Now, how do I get her to spill her guts in half an hour without having to touch her?

I will not touch her. First of all, even though she looks a lot like Kelly, I'm not even remotely attracted to her. And it's not her age that is getting to me. It's her attitude—flirtatious one minute, appalled the next. And then there's Kelly. Kelly doesn't want to see her mother, and there must be a damned good reason. This is the woman who raised Kelly, who helped form her personality. Kelly went through hell on that damned island, but what happened *before*?

Her words haunt me.

I haven't ever been anyone's responsibility other than my own. No one has ever taken care of me, and I don't need anyone to take care of me now.

Time for some investigation. "So," I say, "what do you do for a living, Racine?"

"I'm actually not working," she says. "An unmarried aunt of mine passed away last year, and I've been living off of the estate she left me."

That explains this posh hotel suite. "I'm sorry for your loss."

She nods. "Yes, it was difficult to lose her, but I'm adjusting."

"She must've left you a healthy estate."

"She did. I'm very fortunate."

"What did *she* do for a living?"

"She was a hedge fund manager," Racine says. "A very successful one."

"I'd say she was," I say. "If you can afford Dom Perignon."

"They say money can't buy happiness," Racine chuckles. "But it sure is fun trying."

"Is that why you want to see Kelly? To help her financially?"

"Of course. And to see her. She's my daughter. My one and only."

"What about her father?"

"Her father's not in the picture."

"Oh?"

Racine says nothing, just drops her gaze to her lap.

She's not going to talk about him, whoever he is.

"Was he ever in the picture?"

"No." She doesn't raise her head.

"What about Kelly? Was he ever in the picture for her?"

"No, he wasn't." This time she raises her head. "I don't talk about him. Not to you, and not to anyone," she snaps.

"All right. I'm sorry to bring up a sore spot."

She turns her frown into a smile. "Don't worry about it. I just get a little testy where he's concerned. I had to raise Kelly on my own, and although I worked as an accountant, things were always tight for us."

"I'm sorry to hear that."

I'm also not quite understanding. If Racine was an accountant, she wasn't wealthy, but she certainly was making enough money for a family of two to live a pretty good life. I sense there's a story there.

"Kelly didn't have it easy," Racine says. "She desperately wanted to play volleyball, but I needed her to work, to help."

Kelly's tattoo. A volleyball surrounded by wilted roses. "That must've been difficult for her."

"It was, the poor thing. I didn't have the money to send her to college, either, so she worked as a waitress at a local diner before..." Racine looks down, sniffling.

But something isn't gelling with her story. The sniffle sounds forced. And I bet—

"Racine, look at me."

She looks up. Her face is peaked, but as I suspected, not one tear glistens in the whites of her eyes.

"I know this must be difficult for you to talk about," I say.

"Yes, it is. I miss her so much, too. That's why I came here. To see her."

"I'd like to facilitate that."

"Would you?"

"Of course. I care about Kelly. I'm watching over her. Why wouldn't she want to see you, Racine?"

She shakes her head, sniffling again. "I wish I knew. I wish I knew so many things."

I nod. *So do I.*

My phone buzzes. It's Buck. "I'm sorry. I'm going to have to take this. Do you mind if I step out into the hallway?"

"Not at all."

I rise, leave the suite. Just to be safe, I walk toward the elevators. "Hey," I say into the phone.

"I got a report in. On Racine Taylor."

"Give it to me. I'm with her now, in her hotel room."

"What the hell are you doing in her hotel room?"

"She wasn't talking. And she's, you know...*into* me, so I thought—"

"Do *not* do that."

"Are you kidding me? I'm not touching her with a ten-foot pole. I'm just going to let her think that I might."

"Whatever, dude. Apparently Racine Taylor came into some money about five years ago."

"Five years ago? She told me it was a year ago. She said her aunt died."

"Did she give you a name?"

"Not yet."

"See if you can get a name out of her, but I'm betting that's not where this money came from. There's a deposit of half a million dollars into her bank account on November fifth five years ago, and then, almost like clockwork, another half mil every three months after that for a year."

"Man."

"Not only that, but somehow she got into some investment portfolio with some hot stocks and made a killing. She's worth about thirty million, Leif."

"That explains the Waldorf and the Dom Perignon."

"Damn."

"I know, right?" I shudder as the thought of Racine selling out her only daughter consumes me. "Do you think there's truth to my theory? That she's the one who sold Kelly out?"

"The timing is a little off. Kelly was taken in May of that year. The first payment didn't come until about six months later."

"Right." I scratch my head. "With Aspen and with Katelyn, payment was immediate, and it was also a lot less than two million dollars. Something's not adding up."

"So I guess we scratch that theory out."

"Yeah." Though the thought still pesters me like a swarm of gnats.

"See what you can find out about her."

"Hey, did she ever work as an accountant?"

"No. In fact, she and Kelly were on food stamps when Kelly was a kid. Looks like she kicked Kelly out of the house when she turned eighteen, before she even graduated from high school. A friend took her in."

My heart hurts. "Are you serious?"

"Totally serious. Kelly's personality is becoming more understandable with everything I find out about this woman."

"I'll say. And we don't even know how Racine treated her."

"I know. So far nothing on that. There will never be anything on that unless social services got involved. If Racine didn't leave any marks on Kelly, and Kelly didn't report her mother, there won't be any record."

"There are other kinds of abuse besides physical," I say. "You and I know that better than anyone."

"For sure. It's a mystery. See what you can find out. I get

the feeling that this woman, Racine, is not at all what she appears to be."

"What she appears to be is a spendthrift who wants to get into my pants," I say. "I *will* get something out of her. I'll be in touch."

"You be careful," Buck says.

"I always am. The Phoenix rises from the ashes, so no need to worry about me."

I end the call, walk back to Racine's suite, and knock.

32

KELLY

Ten o'clock. Only two more hours to go on my shift. So far I've made close to a thousand dollars in tips tonight. I don't want to get impressed with myself, but I am a little bit.

Until my phone buzzes in my pocket.

I check it out as soon as I have a free second.

You're nothing. You will die.

I jerk.

No way.

A few days have passed since my last threatening text, and I was hoping beyond hope that it was over.

My heart rate increases, and my animal comes out.

I text back. *Give it a rest, Brindley.*

This isn't Brindley.

Right. And I was born yesterday.

Another text: *You'll get what's coming to you.*

Then one of my own: *Fuck off.*

However, I'm not nearly as brave as the text portrays me. I call Leif.

"Kelly? You okay?"

"I just got another text."

"All right. Forward everything to me, including the number. I'll get it to Reid for a trace."

"Okay."

I quickly forward all the texts, along with the number.

"Did you get it all?"

A few seconds pass. "Yep, got it all. You need me to come over there?"

"I only have an hour left of my shift. I'm okay. I want to finish my first night."

"All right. You want me to pick you up?"

"No, that's okay."

Except I'm lying. I just told Macy I don't lie. I *do* want him to pick me up. But damn it, I *don't* want him to pick me up. I need to stand on my own two feet. I've been standing on my own two feet for so long, it's who I am. It's who I had to be.

"No. I'm going to get a cab."

"You sure?"

"I just said I was sure, didn't I?" I say with a caustic edge.

Damn, there I go again.

"Hey, I know you're stressed out. About the text and all. Let me come get you."

"I said no!" I end the call.

AN HOUR LATER, I walk outside, half expecting Leif to be there.

When he isn't, a surge of disappointment pounds through me. I mean, he was hired to protect me, right? He should be here.

You told him not to come.

I hear the words in Macy's voice, not my own because it's exactly what she would say, and she would be exactly right.

I told him not to come, so he didn't come.

And you would've given him hell if he'd shown up.

Again, Macy's voice.

And again, right on target.

I hail a cab. When I get home, I head straight to Leif's apartment instead of my own. I knock on the door.

He doesn't respond.

I knock louder and ring the doorbell.

Nothing.

Fine then. Isn't he supposed to be protecting me? Shouldn't he be home?

Maybe he's at my place. He likes to let himself in, after all. I go to my apartment, slide my key, and open it.

"Leif?" I yell out.

Nothing. I walk through the apartment, check the kitchen, then my bedroom and bathroom.

No Leif.

Well, I told him I didn't want him barging into my apartment again.

Except I *do* want him here.

And not solely to protect me.

Last night was...

Everything.

And I don't say that lightly.

Like I told Macy, what I wanted was to be cleansed, but I got so much more than that. I felt, if only for a moment, alive.

And it felt good. Felt so damned good.

I sigh, sit on my couch, and stretch my legs onto the coffee table. I'm tired for sure. It's been a long time since I've waited tables, but I've kept my stamina up with workouts in the gym here in the building. One thing I can say about the women on the island, we were all kept in good shape. We had to be in good shape. They wanted us to run. They wanted worthy prey.

I wish I could forget. I wish the time on the island just never came into my mind. But if I forget about that—about the abuse I suffered on the island—what am I left with?

The abuse I suffered at the hands of my own mother—torturous physical and emotional abuse.

In some kind of warped way, I'm almost glad I was abducted and sent to the island.

At least it got my mind off other things.

But which is worse? To be abused and tortured by someone who's supposed to love you, or by strangers who have no relation to you whatsoever?

I already know.

Which is why it was so strange being on the island. Why none of the other women understood my strange kind of envy. I'm not sure I fully understand it yet. Why did it disturb me so much to be in competition with the others? I didn't want to be chosen, so why did I become angry when someone else was selected over me?

Because I've been yearning for attention my entire life... even the kind of attention that hurts.

It's the only kind I ever got, and I got a lot of it on the island, especially from The Dark One.

I worked through the jealousy. I understand it was wrong, and it was a product of what I've been through in my life.

So maybe...

Maybe it truly *isn't* Brindley who's been sending me those messages.

Maybe it's time to confront her directly.

I can't right now. It's too late and I'm exhausted. But I can find Leif, tell him what I've discovered.

Maybe it's time to be honest with him. To tell him what I've been through. Help him understand why I am the way I am, and that although I still struggle, I've come such a long way.

I want him to know that I'm trying. Because I...

I feel things with him that I've never felt before. And I'm not just talking physical, though the physical was incredible. I feel something more. I'm not sure what to call it, but it's a warm feeling. A good feeling.

An almost...happy feeling.

But *is* it happiness? I have nothing to compare it to. I've never felt happiness before.

I walk back over, knock on Leif's door.

And still...no answer.

33

LEIF

I didn't plan to pull an all-nighter with Buck. We had enough of those in Afghanistan, but at least we're in his cushy apartment that he shares with Aspen, not sweltering in the desert, looking over our shoulders for enemy fire.

"She didn't tell me anything," I say. "I asked her for the name of the aunt who left her the money, and she clammed up quickly."

"So she realized you were after information."

"Not at first. First she accused me of wanting her for her money."

Buck lets out a chuckle.

"Until I explained I didn't want her, money or not. Then she escorted me to the door."

"So it's not that she refused to give you the aunt's name, it's that she wanted something more than you were able to give, and she thought by asking for the aunt's name, you were wanting to know more about where she got her money."

I shrug. "Hell, I don't know. I personally don't think there even is an aunt."

Buck taps busily at his computer, and then he raises his eyebrows.

"What is it?" I ask.

"Actually, there is an aunt. Clementine Taylor, and she *was* a hedge fund manager with Norsemen Funds."

I stop my jaw from dropping to the floor. "You've got to be kidding me."

"I wish I were, but I'm not. Clementine Taylor did exist, and her will was probated in Tucson, Arizona. She did leave an estate of approximately ten million to her niece, Racine Taylor."

"You got the will?"

"Right here in the database."

"I'll be damned."

"She wasn't lying. Her aunt did pass away about a year and half ago. And most of the estate passed through trust and wasn't held up by the probate court at all. So pretty much overnight, Racine Taylor was a rich woman."

"Except she was already a rich woman. Those half-million dollar payments started coming out six months after Kelly was taken."

"Yes, there's that as well. It looks like she got four of those altogether, and now she's worth about thirty million dollars, as we already knew. She got into some good stock buys and increased her wealth, and then she got another cash infusion when Auntie Clem died."

"Okay. So it's still possible she sold her daughter."

"It's possible for sure. The only thing that doesn't make sense is why she had to wait six months for payment and why she was paid such a large sum."

"Right, when the people who took Aspen and Katelyn were paid right away, and not nearly as much."

"Then maybe... Maybe she wasn't involved in her daughter's kidnapping," Buck says. "I truly doubt that Derek Wolf paid in the millions of dollars for these women. Hell, if he did that, he could have probably gotten a few to volunteer."

"Maybe, but not if they knew for sure what they were getting into."

"Of course not, but if you're willing to pay that much, there would be a few biters."

"True enough." I cock my head, my mind racing. "Something's not right between Racine and Kelly. That much is obvious. Why else would she refuse to see her mother?"

"Aspen didn't see her parents at first. It's hard to imagine what these women were thinking. Their mindset."

"It's not that hard to imagine." I gesture to a scar on Buck's arm.

"You and I went through a lot, but we were trained for it. What we went through wasn't pretty—and it's nothing I want to experience again—but we knew what could happen to us out there. The fact that a lot of it *did* doesn't change the fact that it was a risk we consciously took. It was our choice."

"True enough. These women didn't make the choice."

"No, they didn't. They didn't take this risk. It was thrust upon them."

"I guess I can see why Aspen didn't want to see her parents at first. It's humiliating. You and I should know."

"Exactly," Buck says. "But, Aspen did see her parents after a while. In fact, I found her at a train station going to Colorado to see them. When I went after her when she disappeared."

"So she made the choice to see them on her own."

"Right. After a lot of therapy, and after realizing that there was nothing for her to be humiliated about. But with Kelly it's different," he says.

"Yeah, it totally is. I did not get good vibes from Racine at all. She said all the right words, claimed to love her daughter, but her acting left a lot to be desired."

"So you don't believe her?"

"Not only no, but *hell* no. She knew how to sniffle at the right time, how to dab at her eyes. But she was dabbing at dry eyes, Buck. Dry fucking eyes."

"They…"

"Right? So whether she had anything to do with her daughter's abduction or not, they did not have a good relationship. Of that I'm certain."

"There's only one way to find out the truth about that," Buck says.

I nod. "I know. I have to ask Kelly."

"And you know how that will go."

"God, do I. But I have to tell you, I'm understanding her better and better. I don't think she has a nasty streak at all. I think she's just super defensive. She's been hurt her whole life, so now she strikes before anyone can hurt her again."

"Do you plan to hurt her?"

"No. Not intentionally, anyway. So I suppose that means…"

"It means hands off, Phoenix."

"You didn't keep your hands off," I shove back at him.

He doesn't reply. How can he? Until—

"No, I didn't. And I'm glad I didn't, because that lovely lady sleeping soundly in the next room is everything to me."

I nod. "I know, bro."

"You're not feeling something for Kelly, are you?"

"No."

But the lie is bitter on my tongue because the truth is that I *am* feeling something for Kelly. I'm going to have to tamp it down. She's certainly not ready to be with anyone, and in my own way, I'm not either.

No more hanky-panky with Kelly Taylor.

And I'm surprised at how much that thought saddens me.

I rise. "Send me a copy of all the docs you found. I'm going to get some shut-eye. Good night."

"Don't you mean good morning?"

I shake my head and sigh. "Damn. What is it? Eight o'clock already?"

"Seven thirty."

I yawn. "See you, Buck."

"Take it easy, Phoenix."

I leave Buck's, take the elevator down to the fourth floor, and head to my place.

And then I drop my jaw.

34

KELLY

No, mama. Please, not the closet!

But she shoves me inside anyway. "Bad girls sit by themselves in the dark. And you've been a bad girl, Kelly."

I don't bother asking her what I've done.

She won't tell me anyway.

I don't even know.

Was I late coming home from school?

No.

Did I leave a mess at the table? Crumbs when I fixed myself a piece of bread with peanut butter?

That's probably it. I love peanut butter, but it's so sticky. I can't help but get it somewhere. Sometimes she can see the tiniest streak on the counter.

"No, mama, no!"

She grips my shoulders. Shakes me. Violently shakes me.

~

"KELLY!"

I pop my eyes open. For a moment I don't know where I am, and I strike. I kick at the person who's gripping me.

"Damn, that hurt."

Leif.

Leif's voice.

I remember. I decided to wait for Leif outside his door, and I must've fallen asleep.

He's rubbing at his shin.

"What the hell are you doing out here?" he demands.

"Where have you been? I needed to talk to you last night."

"I was out," he says.

A spear of jealousy slices through me, gutting me.

Out? He was out? With a woman? After he and I just…

"You're a pig." I sneer.

"So be it," he says. "Look, I'm exhausted. What do you want, Kelly?"

Why did I come here?

Right. I wanted to talk. I wanted to tell him about my successful first night at work. I wanted to tell him…

About my childhood. About why I am the way I am. I want him to understand me, and I want to understand him.

Except he was out all night fucking another woman, so I'm done here.

"Never mind." I get to my feet, stumbling a little.

He studies me. "Come on. Come inside. I'll make a pot of coffee."

"I don't want any coffee, Leif."

"What do you want then? Because it better be something important for you to stay out here all night. You know how dangerous that was?"

"This building has round-the-clock security."

"Yeah, it does, but nothing is completely foolproof. You're much safer locked behind your apartment door."

"Like you care."

He shakes his head again, sighing again. "I have been up all night, Kelly. I don't have time to repeat myself. If you don't know that I care by now—"

"If you cared, you wouldn't have been out all night in someone else's bed!"

He cocks his head, narrows his eyes. Then he does something completely unexpected. He erupts in laughter.

Fine. I can take a hint. I turn with a huff and walk toward my apartment.

He yanks me back. "You really think that? You think I was with another woman?"

"Yeah, I do."

"Well, you're right."

God, the jealousy. Like a bright red blade cutting into my heart. And then the anger. The kind of anger that starts in the depths of your belly and travels up your spine, ending with rats nibbling at the back of your neck.

The rage, the red rage.

Only this is more intense than anything I felt on the island or anywhere else. This is raw. Not just anger but pain. Torturous pain. I feel like an animal—an animal who's about to lose her mate. And I won't go down without a fight.

I push into Leif, pummeling at his chest.

He pushes me away easily. "No. That's not how you handle anger, Kelly. You're not on the island anymore."

"Damn you."

Then I slide my back against the wall and into a sitting position.

I will not cry. I will not honor this man with my tears.

He sits down next to me, and then he does something weird. He takes my hand. He rubs my palm with his thumb.

"I *was* with another woman last night, and you will never guess who it was."

"I don't care who it was."

"I think you might care about this one."

"Why should I care about any woman that you fucked?"

"Well, one, because I didn't fuck her. And two...because she's your mother."

The rage dissipates.

And fear curls into my belly like a cannonball.

My mother. Still, after all these years, she has the ability to turn me into that scared little girl.

I don't know what to say, so I say nothing.

"She wants to see you."

Still I say nothing.

"What happened between the two of you, Kelly?"

Still I say nothing.

He adds his other hand, massaging my palm and my wrist. "I didn't get a good feeling from her. Not at all. But you may be interested to know that she has a lot of money now."

"I know that."

He lifts his eyebrows. "Oh?"

"Yeah. I found out about it once we were rescued. Some spinster aunt of hers left her some kind of sizable estate. She's not going to give any of it to me."

"She says that's why she wants to see you. So she can take care of you."

"She's lying."

I expect him to deny my accusation. Tell me how wonderful and caring she seemed, and that she truly wants to see me and take care of me, her only daughter.

But he doesn't.

Instead—

"I believe you, Kelly. I believe she's lying."

I turn to him, regard his handsome face. "You... You believe me?"

He lets go of my hand, cups both my cheeks. "I do."

"No one's ever believed me before. I mean, not without knowing..."

"We learn how to read people during our SEAL training. It's very important because we have to rely a lot on instinct and intuition. And what I read in your mother was that her words didn't match up with her actions. Her facial expressions, her emotions."

"Just how much time did you spend with her?"

"I met her at her hotel, and we had dinner. After that, I went to Buck's apartment and we were up all night doing research on her."

"So you didn't..."

He laughs again. "My God, no, Kelly. How could you think that?"

"My mother's an attractive woman."

"She's...pretty, but not attractive."

I scoff. "What's that supposed to mean?"

"It means she has pretty features. But her personality keeps her from being attractive."

"Doesn't that mean the same thing?"

"No. Objectively, I can observe her features, and I can say she's pretty, although her features aren't as fine as yours. You happen to be beautiful."

Warmth surges to my cheeks.

"Attractiveness, on the other hand, requires attraction. And I felt no attraction to her. So to me, she's not attractive."

My cheeks are burning from his touch. "No one's ever explained it to me like that before."

"That's how I see it anyway. You're a beautiful woman, Kelly, and you came from your mother. So of course she's quite pretty in an objective sense. But attractive? Not at all. Beautiful? Not even the same galaxy as you."

He uses one hand to tilt my chin and then brushes his lips over mine. "Now, can I make that coffee?"

I nod.

He rises and pulls me into a stand next to him. I want to melt into him, let him embrace me, but I don't.

Not yet.

Maybe over coffee, I'll tell him about my mother.

That's what I was going to do anyway.

Will he run away screaming?

I can't blame him if he does. I come with a hell of a lot of baggage. But I'm feeling something for this man. A warm and cozy feeling like I'm wrapped in a cashmere shawl and protected from the world.

And I think...

Maybe I am.

35

LEIF

"How was your first night at work?" I ask as I fill the coffee maker with water.

"It was good, actually," Kelly says.

"Are you working again tonight?"

"Actually, I'm not. The restaurant starts the new servers working every other night, to get us used to the hours and being on our feet for so long."

"That's good, since you probably didn't sleep very well in the hallway."

"I don't know. I was in some kind of deep sleep when you shook me."

I look down at my shin. "No kidding. I'm going to have a nice bruise."

"I'm sorry about that."

I'm amazed at how quickly and easily the words *I'm sorry* come out of her mouth, but I choose not to mention it.

"It's all right. You didn't mean to, but no more sleeping in the hallway, Kelly. I mean it."

"You didn't answer your door," she says.

"Have you heard of a little thing called a telephone?"

"Yeah, I've heard of it. But I didn't want to talk on the phone, Leif. I wanted to talk to you in person."

"If you had called me, I could've come home."

"Would you?"

"Of course I would've. You're my job."

Her lips turn into a frown. "Right. I'm your job."

I sigh. "You're more than just a job to me. That's not what I meant."

"It's what you said."

I smile then. "You will be the death of me, Kelly Taylor."

"I don't want to be."

"Then let's make a pact. Here and now. We're going to be nice to each other. We're not going to make assumptions about each other. If we have questions, we will ask. If we don't like the answers we receive, we won't lash out."

"I can't promise I won't lash out."

"Yes you can. You can, and you can mean it."

"All right."

"Good. Now we have an understanding between us. No more lashing out, by either of us. That includes me."

"When have you lashed out?"

"Hundreds of times." I smirk. "All in my head, of course."

She smiles. "I'm a real pain in your butt, aren't I?"

"Yes, you are. But I don't mind you so much." I grab two mugs out of the cupboard. "Tell me about your first night at work."

She rattles on then, talking animatedly—more animatedly than I've ever seen her. "Over a thousand dollars in tips. I can't believe it. And the restaurant pays us the tips in cash. Of course, they also made me fill out a tax form, so it's not like I can keep all of it."

"No, but you can keep about seventy percent of it. That's pretty good for a night's work."

"Yeah, absolutely. Especially since I don't have any expenses. At least not yet."

"The Wolfes will let you stay here as long as you need to."

"I know that, but I hate taking other people's money. I hate taking help. I've been on my own since the day I turned eighteen, and I—"

"Since the *day* you turned eighteen?"

I know her story. Her mother kicked her out of the house when she turned eighteen before she was finished with high school. But I want to see if she'll tell me. Confide in me.

"Well, yeah. Aren't most people on their own at eighteen?"

"It's the age you become an adult. But I get the feeling there's more to your story."

"When you were researching my mother... Just how much did you find out?"

"I found out the two of you were on food stamps when you were a kid. I found out that there are no records regarding your childhood, meaning social services was never called."

She looks down.

I tip her chin up. "You can tell me, Kelly. Please. Tell me."

"You'll think less of me."

"Why would I? No child is responsible for anything that happens to her. It's all on your mother, Kelly. Every bit of it."

"That's not true. Sometimes kids can be bad."

"Absolutely. When I misbehaved, I was punished. But there's a difference between punishment...and abuse."

She swallows. "I'm not sure I know that difference."

"I know, and I'm so sorry about that. I don't know what

your mother put you through, but I promise you were never that bad."

"But I was. I must have been." She melts into me, burrows her head into my chest.

She doesn't cry, or at least not any sobs that I can hear. Perhaps she's crying silently, and when she sniffles, I know.

I push her away slightly, so I can look into her glistening eyes.

"Whatever happened, I promise you that none of it was your fault."

"I thought I was done crying over her."

"You are. She doesn't deserve your tears. But you know who does deserve them? The little girl that you were. The little girl that, in some ways, you still are."

"I want to tell you," she says. "I want to tell you everything."

"I'll be happy to listen."

"But I can't, Leif. It's just too painful to talk about it. I've talked about it so much to Macy and my therapists on the island. I feel like I'm all talked out. And I know exactly what you'll say. You'll be horrified, disgusted, and you'll wonder how such a person could even exist. All things I used to wonder myself, until I went to the island and I realized my mother wasn't the only evil in the world."

"Oh, baby." I kiss the top of her head. "Evil is everywhere. You've seen it, and so have I."

"If you've seen what I have, you have my sympathy."

"I haven't seen exactly what you've seen," I say, "but I've seen enough. And I know what happened to you was far worse than anything that happened to me. Kelly, if I could wave a magic wand and make it disappear, I would. I'd give up everything if I could make you happy."

She burrows into my chest once more, and this time her sobs aren't silent.

I'm not sure why I said those words.

But the truth of them envelops me like the warm sun.

I would do anything to make this woman happy.

It hits me like a bolt of lightning.

I've fallen in love.

I've fallen in love with a woman who's not ready to receive love.

It means hands off, Phoenix.

Buck's words... But I didn't keep my hands off when I should have, and now... Now I'm a fucking goner.

I'll go slowly. Is what I'm feeling truly love, or just a strong need to protect her? To protect her from everything she's been through and keep her safe so nothing like that will ever happen again?

Perhaps that's all it is.

I can't be in love with her, not after only a couple of days, during most of which she was yelling at me.

Of course, the sex was amazing. But that's just chemistry. Chemistry between two very needy people.

She probably didn't pay any attention to my words anyway. The poor woman has been destroyed, and now she's putting herself back together.

All the women on the island went through the same thing, but most of them had been ripped from lives that were good. They were succeeding.

Kelly was ripped from a life that never gave her any happiness. Any love.

Poor sweet Kelly.

Kelly only knows how to fight back.

Maybe that's why I was given this assignment. Not just to

protect Kelly, but to show her she's worthy. That she doesn't always have to come out fighting like a cornered wolf.

I kiss the top of her head once more. "You want some breakfast?"

She shakes her head, sniffling against my shirt.

"What can I do for you then, baby?"

She looks to me then. Tears streaking her face, her nose red. "Take me to bed. Please."

36

KELLY

He smiles, and my heart surges.

"Are you sure?"

"Very."

"I wish I could promise you something more than this morning," he says.

"I'm not asking for more."

And I'm not. I don't know that I'm ready, and he and I don't know each other very well.

I've never let myself know another person.

I want to know Leif. I want to know him as more than a protector, even as more than a lover.

At this moment, though, what I need is to capture that feeling again. The feeling of being cleansed, being whole. The only time I've ever felt that was when I was with Leif.

He kisses my cheek, and then he leads me to his bedroom.

His bed of course hasn't been slept in. It's kind of endearing that he makes his bed. Or the Wolfes probably hired a maid for him.

"I don't want this to be just sex, Kelly," he says.

"What do you want it to be?"

"I don't know yet, but I want you to know this isn't just sex to me. I don't do that. I don't have indiscriminate sex."

"Even when you were overseas? On tour?"

"Especially not then. We were working. We were always watching our backs."

"You didn't meet anyone?"

"No one I wanted to have sex with. Buck did. He met a woman named Amira."

"You mean he was in love before Aspen?"

"He was, but Amira died. She was killed by a suicide bomber."

I frown. "Oh. I'm sorry."

"But he's okay. He and Aspen are so perfect for each other."

"I don't think I'll ever be perfect. Not for anyone."

"No one is perfect," Leif says. "Least of all me."

He seems pretty perfect to me, but the fact that he met with my mother last night doesn't help his case. I have so many questions, but they fall to the wayside as I look into his beautiful blue eyes.

"You're so gorgeous, Kelly." He threads his fingers through my hair and then trails one down my cheek. "But I don't have sex with just anyone. A lot of the guys did overseas. It was an escape, and we needed an escape."

"What did you do to escape?"

"Slept mostly, when I could. I'm not saying I was celibate while I was there. But I wasn't like some of the guys. Sex for the sake of sex has never done much for me."

My heart lurches. That means the sex he had with me meant something. A spark of joy hits my heart. At least I think that's what it is. I mean something to him. Something more than just someone to screw.

And that makes me…

I think it makes me happy.

He lowers his mouth to mine and kisses me.

It's a gentle kiss—so different from the raw and passionate kisses we've shared before. And I like it. I like his soft lips sliding over mine, his velvety tongue inching slowly into my mouth.

But the gentleness doesn't last long.

A groan emanates from him, and the kiss deepens. This is the kiss I remember. The feral kiss. The intense kiss. The kiss that makes my whole body sizzle and shoots flaming arrows between my legs.

I return his kiss, and emotion whirls around me and through me and over me and under me. So much emotion that I don't have any context for.

Emotions I don't recognize… Except that I do.

This man accepts me. Understands why I come out fighting. Wants me to know I no longer have to do that.

And I wonder…

I wonder if I found something I was never looking for. Something I wasn't sure existed.

Then the thoughts morph into pure feeling—those emotions I have no name for. Those physical sensations that I *do* have names for but that I've never felt.

I push him away, breaking the kiss so I can gasp in a deep breath.

His eyes are blue fire, and he scorches me with his gaze. "Take off your clothes, Kelly. Take them off quickly."

I got so tired of obeying the men on the island, and I only did so when I had no other choice.

I fought more than anything. I fought and I disobeyed and I swore to God I would never obey another man.

Yet something in me wants to obey Leif.

So I undress.

I undress quickly as his eyes widen with appreciation.

When I'm standing before him naked, trembling slightly, he kneels before me, looks up at me, and then slides his tongue between my legs.

I gasp as electricity courses through my body. He touches my clit, and already, I want to explode.

I fist my hands in his hair, tangling my fingers in his soft strands, and then pulling, pulling his hair, and then pushing his mouth onto me.

He tongues my pussy, sliding through my folds, and then nipping at my clit. He's still fully dressed, and more than anything I want to see him, look at his beautiful body, touch every part of him.

But maybe not more than anything, because I'm standing, standing at the precipice, as he continues to lick me.

Until—

I jump.

I jump into the beautiful oblivion that is the orgasm pulsing through me.

I grind into his mouth, moving with him, undulating my hips, as my body convulses, shatters, as rivers of boiling nectar flow through me and culminate in my core, right in my pussy as he's still licking me.

I say words, but I don't know what they are. They're unintelligible, but they flow out of me, out of my mouth and throat.

He looks at me again, and then, finally, when I begin to

come down, I drop my head, open my eyes, meet his blue gaze.

His chin is glistening, his eyes still on fire.

"Again," he growls.

As if his mere words strike obedience into me, I soar again, this time landing among clouds—light fluffy warm clouds, and this climax is less hectic, more tender.

I continue to fly as he licks me, and I lose count of how many times I begin to flow downward but then soar again. My body is shuddering, and my legs have turned to jelly.

As if reading my mind, Leif scoops me up and lays me down on the bed.

My legs are so spread, and though I would love for his tongue to tantalize me more, what I really need is that huge cock of his burning through me.

My eyes are closed, but I open them when he commands me to.

"Good," he says. "I'm going to undress now. I want you to watch me. I want to see your reaction to every part of me."

Not a hardship for sure. My head turned, I watch as he stands before me, peeling the clothes from his body.

His blue-and-white button-down shirt is wrinkled, probably from staying up all night working with Buck. He unbuttons it slowly, and though I want him to go quicker, I can't help but be mesmerized at every inch of new flesh that is revealed.

I remember.

I remember his smooth porcelain skin, his broad shoulders, his tanned nipples, and his glorious abs.

When he finally parts the shirt, slides it off his shoulders, and throws it to the floor, I suck in a breath as he fiddles with his belt.

Once it's unbuckled, he unzips his fly and kicks his shoes off before he slides the jeans over his hips.

He wears boxer briefs, and they're light blue, nearly matching the color of his eyes. Once his jeans are history he toes off his socks. Then he slides his thumbs under the waistband of his boxer briefs.

My body throbs.

Down go the boxer briefs, and his huge and majestic cock springs forward, so ready.

And I'm so ready *for* it.

He grabs his jeans, pulls out a condom, and quickly sheaths his cock.

Within another second, he's on top of me, hovering over me, the head of his dick teasing my clit.

I could explode again. I could shatter so easily, but I hold myself back. My body is spent already, and what I want—what I really, *really* want—is to feel him slide inside me.

"Are you ready for me?" Leif's voice is low and raspy.

"God, yes," I breathe out on a sigh.

"I'm going to sink into your pussy, Kelly."

"Please..."

"Look at me. Watch me as I sink my cock into you."

Does he want me to look in his eyes? Or between us, at our joining?

I choose his eyes. His beautiful blue eyes. I meet his gaze, and I don't let go.

And with one smooth thrust, he enters me.

Such fullness. Such completion.

Again he burns through me as if cleansing me.

Is this what I need? To be cleansed every time? Or can I just accept that I like this feeling? That I like...*him*?

He pulls out and pushes back in, and then again.

Each time he pulls out, I want to whimper at the loss, but he thrusts back in hard each time, and that feeling of fullness, of completion, drugs me.

It's a high. A high from the feeling of him inside me.

I never want it to end.

Never could I imagine enjoying sex the way I do with Leif. After so much abuse through so much of my life, I never imagined I could want this. Feel this. Revel in this.

He fucks me. He fucks me and he fucks me and he fucks me.

And I realize I don't need another orgasm.

All I need is this.

Leif, inside me, making me complete.

37

LEIF

I won't last much longer, and I would love for Kelly to come again, but she shows no signs of it. I could slide my hand between our bodies, massage her clit. That would get her going.

But her face is beautiful, serene. Her lips are slightly curved into a Mona Lisa smile. Her gaze hasn't wavered from mine, and I can't look away.

Something hypnotic is happening between us, as if our eyes are locked on each other.

And the more I thrust—the more I come closer and closer to release—the stronger the hypnosis between us becomes.

Thrust. Thrust. Thrust.

And then—

"My God!" I plunge into her, letting go.

Each pulse from my cock radiates through me, and the climax both relaxes and tenses me.

Feelings of utter joy spill into me, but it's more than that. It's like a lightning strike, but instead of being harmful, it's transcendent, unparalleled. Perfect in so many ways.

Lightning is struck between Kelly and me.

My life will never be the same.

I don't want to pull out of her, so I stay—our bodies and our gazes joined—for a few timeless moments.

When I finally need to rest my arms, I roll off of her, so sad at the loss of her warmth around me.

I sigh, the hypnosis between our gazes finally releasing.

I roll onto my back, close my eyes, my arm over my forehead.

And I drift away.

I drift away into peaceful slumber.

MY EYES POP open at the sound of my cell phone ringing. I jerk upward, still naked in my bed.

"Kelly?"

But she's gone. The space next to me is empty. Perhaps she's in the bathroom, or she went out into the kitchen or living room.

I rise, grab my cell phone out of the pocket of my jeans. It's Buck.

"Hey," I say into the phone.

"Phoenix, I'm glad I caught you."

"What's up?"

"Aspen and I have to leave town for a few days."

"Everything okay?"

"Yeah, everything's fine, but her mom has to go in for some routine surgery, and she wants to be there."

"What kind of surgery?"

"She broke her wrist, and she's going to need some help

around the house. Her father said we didn't need to come, but Aspen wants to be there."

"I totally understand. Have you notified Reid?"

"Yeah. Everything's a go. But it may increase the workload on you for the next couple of days."

"I've got my hands full with Kelly," I say.

"Right." Buck laughs. "And with her mother."

"Her mother's a nonissue as far as I'm concerned. At least for me. What other work is Reid talking about?"

"Just the stuff you and I would normally do together. I'll be back as soon as I can. I'm only going to go for a few days, just to support Aspen while her mom has the surgery. Once they're all set up in the house, I'll return here and Aspen can stay as long as she's needed."

"So this is your honeymoon," I laugh.

"We'll have a real honeymoon. I promised Aspen, and I promised myself. But for now, this is what Aspen wants to do."

"Got it. When are you leaving?"

"We fly out tonight. Have you been able to get any sleep?"

I check my watch. Damn, it's three p.m. "Yeah, turns out I got quite a bit of sleep."

"You sound pretty relaxed."

"I am. I suppose I should try to find Kelly."

"How'd her first night at work go?"

"Good. She and I talked about it this morning. I think she's going to do well there."

"That's great. I'm happy for her."

"I am too. And I think, slowly, her attitude is changing. She's realizing she doesn't have to come out fighting in every circumstance."

"Good. It's a hard thing to get over."

"I know. You and I both know, buddy."

"That's no lie. Give me a call if you need anything. Cell phone's on day or night."

"Will do. You have a safe trip." I end the call.

I head into my shower, take a quick one, and then dress. Three thirty. Time to find Kelly. I leave my place and knock on her door.

She answers, her eyes wide. "Hi."

"Hi yourself. Where did you go?"

"Here. You found me, didn't you?"

I push past her and into the apartment. "You might've told me you were leaving."

"I thought I was doing something nice, Leif. You said you'd been up all night working. I wanted to let you sleep."

I smile then. It was a nice thought. "In the future, let me know when you're leaving. So I can say goodbye."

She bites her bottom lip. "In the future?"

"I mean... If we... Fuck it." I close in on her and gently kiss her lips. "Yeah, Kelly. In the future."

"So this wasn't just a one-time thing?"

"First of all, it's been two times." I smile. "And didn't I just explain last night that I don't have sex for the sake of sex?"

"We don't know each other."

"No, we don't, and I'd like to remedy that. Would you like to do something today?"

"I don't know."

"Have you seen any of the sites since you've been here?"

"Not really. I haven't gone out a lot. I've been busy with therapy."

"Therapy isn't twenty-four hours a day, Kelly."

"No, but...I just didn't have any desire to leave."

"What if I take you sightseeing?"

"You told me you're from Texas, Leif. What do you know about New York sightseeing?"

"I've been here off and on for the past several years, working for the Wolfe family. I know where everything is. What's your pleasure? You want to go to the Met? The MoMA? Central Park? The Statue of Liberty? Ground Zero? You name it. We'll go."

"It's already three thirty."

"So?"

"So it's probably too late to go to any of the museums or anything."

"Central Park then?"

"What exactly do you do in Central Park?"

"You walk. You have a picnic. You admire the scenery. You watch the people. There's a zoo, a carousel, boating... Loads of stuff and..."

"And?"

"You enjoy the company of the person you're with, Kelly. Me. You enjoy my company, and I enjoy yours."

"Okay." She shrugs. "Let's go to Central Park."

38

KELLY

I've never been an outdoors person—not after my mother ended my volleyball career. I still played when I could, but I stopped caring so much. Caring only led to hurt.

I tend to stay inside, with the exception of the five years I spent on the island. We were forced to be outdoors during the hunt.

Central Park was never on my bucket list, but Leif and I spend a few hours there, until the sun begins to set. It's huge. But we manage to see Belvedere Castle and Conservatory Pond, and then we walk around the great lawn. It's beautiful and green and the castle is gray and magnificent.

We don't talk a lot, and we don't even hold hands, but I feel content. Content just walking beside Leif in this beautiful area of New York City.

"Getting hungry?" he asks.

"I could eat." I turn to him. "How about you? Have you even eaten today?"

He laughs. "No, I haven't, come to think of it. And I can definitely eat."

We get to the nearest subway stop and head toward the apartment building, stopping at a place called Gianni's Pizza.

"Have you had good old-fashioned New York pizza?" Leif asks.

"Lily brought me a slice from a street vendor once," I say.

"Those can be iffy. Some are terrific and others not so much. Most New York pizza places aren't like restaurants, but Gianni's is, and it's the best I've found. He always finds room for me."

This time Leif takes my hand, and we head into the pizzeria.

"Hey, Leif," a young man says. "Twice in as many days." He nods to me. "Nice to see you again."

"It is? Funny, since I've never been here before." I suppress—or try to—a scowl.

"Oh." The man reddens. "Sorry."

"It's okay, Mikey," Leif says. "You got my table?"

"We're pretty crowded right now, as you can see, but I can always squeeze you in."

"That would be great."

We follow Mikey through the restaurant, which is much bigger on the inside than it looks on the outside. The table truly is in the back, very secluded. A candle gives out some soft light. Normally I'd enjoy the aroma of rustic tomato and cheese, but I'm pissed.

"Will a server even know we're back here?" I ask, not so nicely.

Mikey laughs. "Oh yeah. We have great service. Tell her, Leif."

I raise my eyebrow. "Yeah. Tell me, Leif."

"Service is great," he says. "And the pizza's always great. Plus they make garlic knots to die for."

At that, my stomach lets out a growl, much to my dismay. I'm still busy being pissed.

How long has it been since I had a garlic knot? We used to serve those at the diner. It's been...over five years.

The waiter hands us each a menu and then looks at Leif. "The usual?"

"What's the usual?" I ask.

Mikey laughs. "Leif and his friend Buck come in here and usually get an extra-large with every single meat topping we offer."

"Excluding the anchovies." Leif says. "I don't consider anchovies meat."

Mikey lets out a guffaw.

"Sure," I say. "The usual sounds great."

"You sure?" Leif asks. "It's huge, and they pile on the toppings."

"I'm sure," I grit out.

"In that case, Mike, give us the usual." Leif smiles. "I haven't eaten since yesterday, so I'm freaking starving."

"And to drink?"

"How about a bottle of your best Chianti," Leif says.

I open my mouth to protest but then I close it. Chianti sounds good. I enjoyed the glass I had with the lasagna that Buck made. Plus...I need to take the edge off.

"You got it. Frankie will bring out your water soon."

"How come he took the order himself?" I ask Leif.

"Because he knows what I like," Leif says. "Mikey and I go way back."

"You do?"

"Yeah... We met...in Afghanistan."

"Oh..."

"He was an infantry soldier on the ground. Buck and I... Well, we kind of saved his life."

"You did?"

"Yeah. He was injured, and his platoon left him behind. Buck and I found him, and we got to a MASH unit."

"His platoon left him behind?"

"They were following orders, Kelly. It happens. But it wasn't Mikey's time, and we got him the help he needed."

"I see."

My anger begins to dissipate. So Leif brought another woman here two days ago. It was probably Terry. Damn her, anyway.

"We were just doing our jobs. Mike got sent home after that, and he began working here. His brother owns the place. Buck and I were kept apprised of his whereabouts, and when we ended up in Manhattan working for the Wolfes, we found him here, along with the best pizza ever."

"So you're a real-life hero," I say.

"I wouldn't put it that way."

"Normally I wouldn't neither," I admit. "I don't find the human race to be particularly heroic. At least not those I've interacted with."

He reaches across the table and grabs my hand. "I'm sorry you feel that way."

"You brought Terry here."

"I did, but only because I forgot to make a reservation for dinner, and Mikey always has a table for me."

"Still..."

"It was nothing, Kelly. I've told you."

"Then why did he have to mention it?"

"Damned if I know. You and Terry don't look anything alike."

"That's for sure."

"You're way more beautiful than she is."

"Do you have to do that?" I ask.

"Do what?"

"Make me feel all...squishy, when I'm trying to be mad at you?"

"If you have to try, I must be doing something right." He reaches across the table and pats my hand. "See? Not all humans are bad."

"I know."

"But I understand what you mean. I've seen some of the worst of humanity myself. But most are good. I hope you're finding that out now."

"It's taken me a long time to accept that. I guess I always feel like someone has an ulterior motive."

"Very few of us have ulterior motives."

"So you don't think Brindley is sending those messages?"

"I don't. I really don't. But if it will make you feel better, I'll go with you to talk to her and we can confront her about it."

"You would do that?"

"Of course. My job is to protect you. To do what you need."

I pull my hand away. "Right. Just doing your job."

He said he doesn't have sex for the sake of sex. But I *am* his job. And sex is what I needed.

He was just doing his fucking job.

I don't say much until the pizza arrives, along with some garlic knots.

Leif nods to me, so I take a garlic knot and place it on the small plate. Our server loads a gargantuan slice of pizza onto my bigger plate.

"You all know how to eat our pizza, right?" she says.

"Absolutely, Frankie," Leif says. "I'll be glad to teach my companion."

"Yes, he'll teach me," I say, forcing a smile. "It's his *job*."

"STILL NOT TALKING TO ME?" Leif says as we enter the apartment building.

I simply shrug.

We whisk past security to the elevators. Then he grips my shoulders, forcing me to look at him.

"Kelly, I don't know what the hell I did, but—"

"Was sex with me part of your job?" I demand.

He cocks his head, drops his jaw. "Is that what this is about?"

"You said you'd go talk to Brindley with me because it's your job. You said you'd do whatever I need you to do, because it's your *job*."

"It might interest you to know that my job description with the Wolfes does not include sex with you."

"Yeah? It was what I needed at the time."

"I didn't make love to you because you needed it."

"Make love?" I scoff. "I detest euphemisms, Leif."

"Kelly, can we table this discussion? I already texted Brindley and told her we were coming to talk to her tonight. Please?"

I huff. "Fine. Let's go talk to the bitch."

I want to take back the word *bitch*, which is unlike me. I *am* changing, and though Macy and everyone else seem to think it's for the better, I wonder if it truly is. I'm vulnerable now. So damned vulnerable—and I'm the most vulnerable to the man standing next to me.

The elevator arrives, and we get in, heading up to the fifth floor.

Brindley was moved from the fourth to the fifth floor at my request, and she was glad to go. Once the elevator arrives, we walk to her apartment—512.

"You sure about this?" Leif asks.

"Yes. I'm sure. Are you? Sure that this is part of your job description?"

He sighs and rolls his eyes. "Let's get this over with." He knocks on the door.

The door opens, and Brindley stands there. She's a petite young woman with brown hair and brown eyes, a girl-next-door look about her. Very pretty, but not classically beautiful. A spray of freckles dances across her nose.

"Hello. Are you Leif?"

"I am. And of course you know Kelly."

I don't say anything.

"Come on in. I put out some cheese and crackers."

Cheese and crackers? I'm full of pizza. And I hate the fact that the pizza was as delicious as Leif said it would be.

Leif steps back to let me enter first. I hold back my scoff. He is a gentleman, but then again... It's all part of his *job*.

"Please have a seat." Brindley gestures to her small living room.

I take a seat on the couch, and Leif sits next to me. Brindley pours us each a glass of water, setting them in front of us. "Help yourself to some food."

"That's kind of you, Brindley," Leif says, "but Kelly and I just ate a huge dinner."

Brindley's cheeks redden. "I should've known. It is around dinnertime. But my mother always taught me to offer visitors food and drink."

I resist an eye roll.

"You know why we're here," Leif says. "Kelly is still convinced that you have something to do with the messages she's receiving."

"I swear I haven't." She shakes her head, her eyes wide. "I would never do anything like that. You can search this place if you want. I have nothing to hide."

"I don't personally believe you're involved," Leif says. "I just don't know how you can convince Kelly."

Sure, Leif. Take her side. Take Terry to your special pizza place. Take care of everyone except me. I'm just your job.

Brindley sits down next to me, which makes me very uncomfortable. I'm just as close to Leif, but I don't want Brindley in that bubble.

"Kelly, I have no idea what you've been through. And I'm so sorry for everything you're still going through. But you have to believe me. I would never put any of you women through any more torment. We've all been through enough."

I cross my arms. "You were only on that island for a few months."

"I know. Still, I was subjected to the same abuse and torture."

"For a lot less time."

"Yes, and believe me, I'm grateful for that. So why would I want to torment any of you?"

"Indeed, why not?" I say with sarcasm.

"Kelly, come on." From Leif.

I look at him.

I look at the handsome man who has made me feel things I never thought I was capable of feeling.

The man whose job it is to protect me.

The Ex-Navy SEAL. And he's damned good at his job. The man who saved Mikey from dying alone, abandoned by his platoon.

Why am I so convinced it's Brindley?

Because I was—*am*—envious of Brindley.

She was subjected to so much less torture than the rest of us were.

She denied it several times, but in my mind, she'd admitted it. I convinced myself Brindley was the culprit because she hadn't suffered as much on the island. Perhaps I never heard fidgeting on my doorknob at night. Perhaps it was all a conjured mechanism to prove to myself that Brindley was behind the texts.

Because I needed someone to blame.

And because...

If it's not Brindley?

Then I don't know who it is.

And that scares me the most of all.

39

LEIF

Kelly stares down at her lap, her hands clasped together. Is she thinking? Is she getting ready to strike?

I don't think she's getting ready to strike because she doesn't think before doing that. If she were going to strike again, she would've already done so.

Then the ding of a text.

Kelly reaches for her small purse and pulls out her cell phone.

Then she gasps.

"What is it?"

"Another one." She hands the phone to me.

You will get what you deserve, you traitorous bitch.

"You're truly off the hook now, Brindley," Leif says.

"Oh my God, is it another one of those texts?" Brindley asks.

I nod, and Kelly stays quiet.

"I'm sorry you got this," I say. "But I swear to God I will protect you. And now... Do you believe that it's not Brindley?"

"Why should I? She could have someone sending them for her."

I sigh. "Kelly... Please."

Finally, she looks up at me, her gorgeous eyes laced with sadness. "Who's doing this to me, Leif? Who? And why?"

"I don't know, baby. But I swear to God we will find out." I turn back to Brindley. "I'm sorry we bothered you."

"It was no bother. I'm happy to have any kind of chance to prove my innocence. I guess it doesn't matter now. Whoever texted Kelly proved it for me."

"Kelly?" I say.

She looks to Brindley. "It's not you, is it?"

"No, it's not. It never was."

I don't expect Kelly to apologize to Brindley, so I rise and offer her my hand. "You want to go home?"

"Yeah." She stands as well, and then she turns to Brindley. "I... I'm sorry."

Brindley drops her jaw.

And I keep from dropping mine.

"I'm just glad my name has been cleared," Brindley says. "I do hope you find out who's doing this to you, Kelly. You don't deserve it. None of us deserves any more pain for the rest of our lives."

Kelly simply nods, and then she walks toward the door. I follow her.

"Thank you for your hospitality, Brindley."

"Any time. Both of you are always welcome here. I get kind of lonely."

"Will you be returning to your family soon?" I ask.

"Sadly, I don't have a family," Brindley says. "I grew up in the foster system. I got kicked out of that when I was eighteen, so with no place to go, I ended up on the streets. In a bizarre way, the island saved me. At least I got enough to eat every day."

Kelly drops her jaw. "I didn't know."

"You didn't ask me."

"You've never talked about it in group therapy," Kelly says.

"You've never talked about your childhood in group therapy either."

Kelly closes her mouth then.

"I'm sorry to hear about that," I say to Brindley. "If you need anything, I'm in the apartment next to Kelly's."

"That's kind of you, but the Wolfe family has made sure I have everything I need. And Macy is a wonderful therapist. To be honest, this is the best home I've ever had. I'm not in any hurry to leave it. Good night."

She closes the door, leaving Kelly and me in the hall.

"I didn't know," Kelly says.

"I know you didn't. Everyone has a story. Everyone is so much more than what they seem on the surface. You are way more than what you seem on the surface, Kelly. Deep down inside you are an amazing person, and I hope one day you see that."

Her lips tremble. "Why are you so nice to me?"

I open my mouth, but she interrupts me.

"It's your job, isn't it?"

"My job is to protect you, baby. Nothing in the job description says I need to be nice to do that."

That actually gets a smile out of her.

But then she looks at her phone, and the sadness returns.

"I don't understand," she says. "Who could be doing this?"

The elevator dings then, and we get on and go down to the fourth floor.

Kelly's phone dings again.

Her lips tremble. "I'm almost afraid to look."

I take the phone from her.

And I widen my eyes as my heart nearly beats right out of my chest.

"What?" Kelly demands. "What is it?"

I love you.

The words don't come out, but I feel them more than ever...along with a raw instinct to protect her. And to take out whoever's threatening her.

Because this last text?

Whoever sent it means business.

READ the conclusion to Kelly and Leif's story in *Phoenix!*

EXCERPT FROM REBEL

The beginning of the story...

Chapter One
Rock

When I was fourteen years old, I tried to kill my father.

The stunt had cost me my freedom. I'd have gladly spent the rest of my life imprisoned as the love slave of a Greek battalion had I been successful. But to be put through hell when the bastard was still alive? So not worth it.

Military school. Not just any military school, but a private academy where millionaires sent their troubled kids to be beaten down, where the rules were that there were no rules. Where survival of the fittest was no longer reserved for the animal kingdom.

I survived.

I grew stronger living through the hell that was Buffington Academy. Secluded in the Adirondacks, the school was home to the most spoiled young men in the world...and the most troubled. After two weeks, I knew I didn't belong there, but I spent four years in that hellhole.

Those years made me wish for juvie.

But no, my parents didn't turn me in. Instead...Buffington.

I spent those years plotting my father's demise, but of course by the time I turned eighteen and released myself, I knew better. I'd learned my lesson. My father wasn't worth it. Trying to take him out had cost me four years of my life.

Even so, I dreamed of his death. It was no less than he deserved.

But when it finally happened, I was totally unprepared.

"Dad's dead," my brother Reid said into the phone when I answered.

I froze, as if ice water had replaced the blood in my veins.

"Did you hear me?"

"Yeah. Yeah. What happened?"

"We're not sure yet. But I have to ask you, bro..."

"What?"

"Were you anywhere near Dad's penthouse last night?"

"Are you fucking kidding me?"

"Someone shot him in the head in the penthouse."

I couldn't help a chuckle. Most guys might freak out hearing this kind of news. Not me. The bastard had it coming.

"They're going to get in touch with you," Reid continued.

"I'm at my cabin, Reid. And by the way, you don't sound too broken up."

"None of us are. He was a bastard. That's public knowledge."

"So why the interrogation? There're a thousand people who probably wanted him dead."

"True, but Dad sent you away when you were so young.

The cops are going to think you might be getting back at him."

"Don't you think I'd have done something before now?"

"Whatever, man. Still, Riley, Roy, and I need to know. Did this in any way involve you?"

"I just told you. I'm home."

"You could have hired it out."

Seriously? I'd been a model citizen since I left Buffington —well, maybe not model in the sense of perfect, since I'd been arrested in a biker brawl once, but I hadn't started it and the charges were dropped. I'd driven after too many drinks a few times, but I hadn't gotten caught. I'd made my own money, never stole a dime. And never took one penny from that motherfucker who'd fathered me. Not that he would have given me any. I had a few biker buds who might have been able to handle a contract on a human life, but I'd have never asked.

The asshole warranted better than a paid hitman who bore him no ill will. He deserved to be taken out by someone he'd wronged, someone who could look into his cold eyes so he knew who was doing the deed.

There were a ton of us out there.

"I didn't," I told my brother. "Trust me. I had nothing to do with it. But I'm glad the asshole's dead."

"None of us are crying, like I said." Reid sighed through the phone line. "Thank God."

"Relieved, are you?"

"Of course. You're my big brother. I don't want you rotting in prison for the rest of your life."

I hadn't seen my brothers and sister in years. Reid was the only one who kept in touch with me regularly. I heard from

Roy and Riley every once in a while. Roy didn't keep in touch with anyone, and Riley had her own issues.

"I won't be. I was out on a ride last night with buddies who can vouch for me. I got in around one a.m."

"They think the murder occurred around four this morning. You couldn't have gotten here by then."

"Plus the fact that I'm still in Montana right now."

"Yeah. Right. I'm not thinking straight." Reid cleared his throat. "You need to get on the next flight to New York."

"Fuck that. I'm not coming home."

"You have to. The cops want to talk to you."

"There's this little thing called a phone."

"Damn it, Rock. You need to come home."

"Burn him and be done with it. You don't need me for that."

"We haven't made any funeral arrangements yet."

"What do you need me for, then?

"The attorneys are reading Dad's will tomorrow morning."

"Why the hell should I care? You know he didn't leave me a damned penny."

"It specifies that we all have to be present. They won't read it without you there."

"You've got to be kidding me." The bastard was going to rub my nose in it from the grave. All his billions...and I'd get nothing.

Not that I cared.

Much, anyway.

"Sorry," Reid said. "But it'll be good to see you, bro. I've... missed you."

Truthfully, I'd missed him as well. He was my youngest brother, and he and I had been close once. Roy, who fell between us, was a classic introvert who'd spent most of his childhood in his room painting or reading. That left Reid to be my primary playmate, even though he was five years younger. Riley hadn't come around until I was eight and Reid was three.

"All right. I'll get a flight."

"I'm one step ahead of you. I'm emailing you your confirmation. Pack a bag. Your flight leaves out of Helena in three hours."

Chapter Two
Lacey

The estate of Derek Paul Wolfe...

I'd drafted the last updates to his last will and testament just three weeks earlier. He'd made some changes that puzzled me, but I was an attorney. My job was to do what the client wanted as long as the law allowed it.

And the law allowed a person to bequeath whatever he wanted to whomever he wanted with whatever contingencies he wanted.

I fiddled with my hair. I was about to meet Derek Wolfe's ex-wife and children. His longtime live-in lover, ex-supermodel Fonda Burke, would probably show up as well.

I'd never met any of them, but I'd seen plenty of photos. They were all spectacular, as anyone descended from or associated with Derek Wolfe was bound to be.

He had a reputation as a wolf—no pun intended—in the boardroom and the bedroom. Not that I'd know, though he'd tried to lure me to his bed more than once. Admittedly, I'd considered it, even though he was thirty years my senior. The man was gorgeous.

His sons were even more gorgeous. At least the two

younger ones were. I'd never seen so much as a photo of his oldest son, Rock. His daughter, Riley, was quickly replacing Fonda Burke as the most successful supermodel of all time—a fact I was sure perturbed the latter more than a lot.

I needed caffeine. Actually, I needed a shot of tequila, but coffee would have to suffice. I couldn't meet the children of Derek Wolfe with alcohol on my breath.

Today I'd deliver some news that none of them could possibly be expecting.

* * * *

I sat at the head of the table in the conference room. I'd only been made a partner during the last year, so when my mentor, Robert Mayes, had given me the Derek Wolfe estate file, presumably at the client's request, I'd been more than a little flabbergasted, but large estates were my specialty, so I'd dived right in.

To my right sat Constance Larson Wolfe, blond and beautiful and botoxed, perfect "first wife" material. She and Derek had been divorced for the last five years, and she'd been living the high life on her spousal maintenance. She wouldn't like what was in the document I held before me, but nothing could be done about that.

Next to her was Riley Wolfe, supermodel extraordinaire, and Derek's only daughter. Dark hair and eyes, definitely a winter type, though she modeled during all the seasons. She was in demand and was fast accumulating her own fortune.

To Riley's right was Roy Wolfe, the middle brother. He was an artist—though not a starving one—by trade, living off his hefty trust fund. He had the most perfect face of all the brothers, a male version of his baby sister. His long hair was as silky and shiny as hers was, though it was pulled back in a low ponytail. He was known as somewhat of a recluse.

Next to him was Reid Wolfe, the youngest brother, who sported the signature Derek Wolfe dark hair—all of the children did—but instead of brown eyes, his were a searing blue that held a seductive look, even when he was sitting and waiting for his father's will to be read. Small wonder he was so popular with the ladies. He was a playboy of the first order, always with a new woman on his arm.

Fonda Burke sat on my left. Still a beautiful woman at forty-two with flaming orange hair and striking green eyes, she had much to look forward to. She wouldn't be happy with the reading of the will.

None of them would be.

We sat quietly, waiting for the missing person.

Rock Wolfe—the oldest child of Derek and Connie Wolfe.

The rebel.

Rock had a troubled past, though no one actually knew the facts other than his family, and I wasn't sure they even knew. Derek had made no secret of his animosity toward his firstborn son.

We sat, no one speaking. Until Reid said, "He should be here by now. His flight got in an hour and a half ago, and I told him to come straight here."

"Rock has always been on his own time schedule," Connie Wolfe said. "That's part of his charm."

Then two harsh knocks on my door. "Come in," I said, expecting my assistant, Charlie.

Instead, in strolled a man who could only be the elusive Rock Wolfe.

While his brothers' hair was sleek and combed into place, Rock's dark tresses were wavy and unruly, falling below his shoulders. His jawline was sculpted and laced with black stubble, and his nose slightly crooked, clearly had been broken at least once. His lips were full and beautiful. And his eyes... A green so clear and powerful a person could get lost in them.

I had to break my gaze away from his magnificently handsome face to notice his wardrobe. While his brothers were clad in Armani suits and ties, Rock wore Levi's that accented his ass and thighs to perfection. A black leather motorcycle jacket—over gorgeously broad shoulders—and black boots completed his ensemble.

He'd at least put on a button-down black shirt for the occasion, open at the neck, a few dark chest hairs peeking out.

"Please have a seat, Mr. Wolfe," I said, willing my voice not to crack. "Everyone else is here, so we can get started."

He glared at me. "Who the hell are you?"

"I'm Lacey Ward, your father's estate attorney."

"Lacey, huh?"

"Yes."

Charlie sat down at the opposite end of the table to take notes. She glanced at me with an "I'm sorry" look.

Rock chuckled and took the seat next to Reid. "Did your mother name you after the lingerie she was wearing the night you were conceived?"

Reid nudged him. "Jesus Christ, Rock."

My cheeks warmed. This was Derek Wolfe's son all right, clear down to the douchebag gene. *Stay professional, Lace.*

"My name isn't up for discussion right now. Since we're all here, let's get to your father's will."

"I can't fucking wait," Rock said with a touch—okay, a huge amount—of sarcasm.

I cleared my throat and began.

Chapter Three

Rock

Lacey Ward was fucking hot.

Oh, she tried to hide it in her navy-blue blazer and tight-ass high-necked blouse, her dark blond hair pulled into a high ponytail so tight that her facial muscles could barely move, and her unglossed lips pressed into a straight line, but I knew the type.

A fucking tomcat in the sack.

I could tell by her eyes. They were big, blue, and vibrant, and they looked me over as if I were a hunk of USDA prime beef tenderloin.

Yup, a tomcat.

Not that I'd ever know. Hell, not that I cared.

I was here for one reason only—so my mother and siblings could hear the contents of the shithead's will. I already knew he'd left me a fat lot of nothing.

And I didn't care one fucking bit.

Lacey Ward's voice had a rasp to it. A sexy rasp. It wouldn't be a hardship to listen to her for the next few hours. Hell, I didn't even need to listen to the words. I knew what they'd be anyway.

Rock gets nothing.

Fine with me.

"Section Five, distribution of personal property," Lacey said. "All of my mother's jewelry in my possession and in the safe deposit box at First National Bank is hereby bequeathed to my daughter Riley Doris Wolfe."

No surprise there.

"My automobiles, except for the Tesla and the Porsche, are bequeathed to my sons, Roy and Reid Wolfe, with Roy, as the older, to have the first choice. They will then choose alternately. The Porsche is bequeathed to my daughter, Riley Wolfe."

His cars. Daddy's pride and joy. He loved those damned cars more than he ever loved any person in his life, least of all me.

I stopped listening. I sat back, closed my eyes, and basked in the rhythm of Lacey's sexy voice.

Yeah, Rock. Fuck me good, baby. Pound that hard cock into me...

My groin tightened. Hell, I didn't care. Just get this day over with.

That's it, baby. Fuck me. Make me come...

Damn, she'd look good on the back of my bike, that blond hair flowing out of a helmet. Yup, I was a helmet man. No point in splattering my brains all over the place. Now that I had a life I enjoyed, I wanted to keep it that way.

I hated Manhattan. I wanted to go back to Montana, where the sky was big and blue and everything was open. New York was so closed in. And it smelled. Even in this posh Manhattan office, the stench of the streets still wafted in the air.

I looked around. My brother Roy was looking down at his lap, while Reid was ogling Lacey. Not that I blamed him. He'd probably fucked her already.

A spear of jealousy hit my gut. Why? I didn't know. So what if he'd fucked her? Reid fucked anything in a skirt.

My little sister, Riley, sat next to my mother.

Riley... The sight of her brought it all back. We weren't close, and I was sorry about that. I'd been protecting her that day, but she didn't know that, and I could never tell her.

Then of course...Mommie Dearest.

Constance Wolfe.

Bitch extraordinaire, who'd had no issue with turning a blind eye to her husband's extracurricular activities.

My gaze floated back to Lacey Ward. I closed my eyes again and sighed. This was going to be a long day.

"Section Seven, real property..."

Can I please doze off now? The villa in Tuscany, the ski chateau in Aspen, the loft in Paris. Who needed all that shit? I had my small cabin in Montana, a Harley, and a job doing construction. It kept me fit and paid well, enough to pay my mortgage, keep food in my belly, and gas in my bike. I got to spend a lot of time outdoors. Who needed anything else?

Man, that voice...

Sink that big cock into me, Rock. Yeah, just like that...

Then...

Silence.

My eyes shot open.

Five gazes, belonging to my mother, my siblings, and my father's current slut, were darting arrows straight toward me.

Chapter Four

Lacey

Had Rock Wolfe heard what I said?

I'd expected a major outburst.

The outburst came, but not from Rock.

"You've got to be kidding me," Reid said, standing. "You misread that."

I cleared my throat. "I assure you I didn't."

"Dad couldn't have agreed to that," he said.

"It's outrageous," Connie Wolfe said, her perfect lips a straight line. "Nothing to me? Or my other children?" she added, most likely as an afterthought.

"You're the *ex*-wife, Connie," Fonda said, smirking, "in case you've forgotten."

"I'm the mother of Derek's children," Connie snarled back at her, "and I don't recall hearing your name being read either."

These two were about to have a mega-catfight if I didn't regain control of this meeting. Roy remained silent, but that didn't surprise me. He was known to be quiet. Riley, however, looked distant, as though she were somewhere else entirely.

I cleared my throat. "These were Mr. Wolfe's wishes. I have all the notes in my office, and I recorded all of our meetings."

"We'll just contest it," Connie said. "Reid has been Derek's right-hand man for years. None of this makes any sense."

Right. That viper wasn't concerned about Reid at all. Her gravy train had ended with Derek's death, and she was far from happy about it.

"You may certainly contest the will, Mrs. Wolfe," I said, "but you'll be wasting your time and money. Your ex-husband made his wishes very clear."

Constance Wolfe darted her gaze to her oldest son, who was staring at me wide-eyed. "Rock, don't you have anything to say about all of this?"

"Why should I?" he asked.

Connie shook her head and scoffed. "You haven't changed a bit."

"That's a good thing, from where I'm sitting," Rock said, smiling. "Why the hell is everyone staring at me?"

"Uh...because our father just mandated that you become CEO of Wolfe Enterprises," Reid said.

Rock cocked his head, one eyebrow rising. "Excuse me?"

"Christ, Rock, haven't you been listening?"

"Of course I haven't been listening. Do you think I give a rat's ass what the bastard put in his will? He only mandated that I be here so that he could rub my nose in the fact that I was getting nothing. What he didn't count on was me not giving a flying fuck."

"Rock," Roy said softly. "Dad just put the fate of our birthright in your hands."

* * * *

Ten minutes later, I found myself in my office with a rabid Rock Wolfe.

"I'm out of here," he'd said, standing and heading toward the door.

Charlie had looked at me with pleading eyes, so I'd turned to the family. "I'll take care of this." Then I'd headed out the door after Rock.

Somehow I'd convinced him to follow me to my office.

"What?" He looked at me irately.

"Were you truly not listening to anything I said in there?"

"Honestly? No. I was imagining the two of us fucking."

Warmth spread to my cheeks, and my pulse thumped, despite myself. A torpedo shot between my legs.

I cleared my throat. "I'd like to keep our relationship professional, please, Mr. Wolfe."

"Sure, we can keep it professional. You asked if I was listening. I told you what I was doing instead of listening. Nothing unprofessional there."

Best to ignore him. Rock Wolfe was trouble. Trouble I didn't need in my life at the moment.

I cleared my throat again. Time to cut to the chase.

"Mr. Wolfe—"

"Rock. Mr. Wolfe was that bastard who died."

He wasn't making this easy. "All right. Rock. Your father

just mandated that you move to Manhattan and take your place at the head of his company—rather, *your* company—as chief executive officer."

"What? No way. What the hell is he trying to pull? He hates me. And I don't know anything about his fucking business. I also don't give a shit."

I sighed. "Believe me, I tried to talk him out of this scheme, but he was adamant."

"*You* wrote this thing?"

"That's what he paid me to do."

"Jesus fuck." He sat down in one of the leather chairs across from my desk. "I won't do it, I tell you. I won't. I wouldn't know what I was doing anyway."

I walked around my desk and took a seat, facing him. "You really weren't listening, were you?"

He smiled. God, he was gorgeous. I hated the effect he was having on my body.

"I already told you what I was doing, Lacey Lingerie."

I seethed, despite the tickle between my legs.

"I still bet your mother was wearing lace that night. Where else would you get a name like Lacey?"

"You're one to talk, with a name like Rock."

"My mom was a fan of the old Rock Hudson and Doris Day movies. Riley's middle name is Doris."

"You do know that Rock Hudson was gay, right?"

"Yeah, I do. So what? That doesn't mean everyone named Rock is gay."

"And neither is every Lacey named after undergarments."

He smiled again, but this time he didn't push it.

I cleared my throat. "Your father has left his business interests in Wolfe Enterprises, which, as you know, is a three billion dollar corporation—"

"I haven't seen my father in twenty-some years. I don't know shit."

"All right." I sighed. "Now you know. You are heir to a three billion dollar corporation."

"You're telling me I'm as rich as Bill Gates now?"

"Hardly, but you *are* rich. Once you get into billions, does it really matter?" Indeed, any amount in the billions was incomprehensible to most, myself included.

He sat, stunned, his green eyes wide. "What the hell am I going to do with all of that?"

"It's not solely yours. He left it in equal parts to you, your brothers, and your sister."

"Good. They deserve it."

"But there was a stipulation." I stood. "Didn't you wonder why everyone was staring at you in the conference room?"

"It was obviously my devastating good looks," he said, smiling.

I couldn't fault his observation, even though he was clearly just flirting with me. If I were the type to go for a leather-clad bad boy, I'd be all over Rock Wolfe.

Fortunately, I wasn't that type.

At least that was what I kept telling myself.

"Mr. Wolfe—"

"We've been through that. My name is Rock."

"Rock." I sighed. "The stipulation I'm talking about is this. For you and your siblings to inherit the business holdings at all, you, Rock Wolfe, must move to Manhattan and take your place as CEO of the company. You need to run the company, or it will be sold to the highest bidder."

Chapter Five
Rock

Fucking bastard.

This had to be some kind of a sick joke.

"I assure you it's not," Lacey said, when I mentioned the same. "I tried to talk him out of this. I told him you had no idea how to run a billion dollar company, and that it was irresponsible to put his company in the hands of a son he'd been estranged from for so long, a son who'd never had any experience in business at all."

A son who'd tried to off him once.

But she didn't know that.

"And he didn't listen to you? What the hell kind of lawyer are you? Can't you control your clients?"

She walked around her desk and stood right in front of me, forcing me to look up at her. "It's my job to advise my clients what the law is and what is in their best interests under the law. I didn't feel this decision was in his company's best interest, and I told him so many times. However, the law allows a person to bequeath his property to whomever he chooses with whatever stipulations he chooses. I did my job, Mr. Wolfe."

There she went with the Mr. Wolfe again. She looked cutely irate, her hands glued to her hips and her cheeks flushing a glorious pink.

"Well"—I stood, this time making her look up to *me*—"I won't do it. I don't give a flying fuck about Wolfe Enterprises."

"Do you give a flying fuck about Roy, Reid, and Riley?" she asked adamantly.

I sat back down with a plunk.

Roy, Reid, and Riley.

Of course I gave a fuck. They were my brothers and sister. I'd protected them as best I could before I'd been sent away.

"Well?" she asked again.

I closed my eyes. "Yes."

"Then you don't have a choice," Lacey said. "They lose their inheritance if you don't do as the will stipulates."

"You mean as my bastard father stipulates," I said. "He's coming after me from the grave, the son of a bitch."

She placed her hand on my shoulder. The gesture was caring, but it ignited a spark under my skin.

"He is. But if you don't do this, Rock, your siblings will suffer. They won't get their share of the business."

"They still got plenty from that will," I said. "I was lucid when I heard that Reid and Roy got all the cars, Riley all the jewels. They can still live the high life. Who got the home in Tuscany? Aspen?"

"You did."

I stood. "What the fuck?"

"You got all the real property, including the Manhattan penthouse."

"Well, that's easy enough to remedy. I'll give all the real estate to my siblings."

"You can't."

"Why the hell not?"

"It's all part of the stipulation. You take the reins at Wolfe Enterprises, or everything is sold to the highest bidder."

"What about cash on hand?"

"There isn't any. Nothing of substance, anyway. Your father died without any liquid assets. It's all tied up in real estate and business."

"You've got to be kidding me."

"I wish I were. I'm sure your siblings wish the same thing."

"I can't do this, Lacey. I just can't. I have a life, damn it. A life I love in Montana. I'm free there. Free to do as I please. Take off on my bike whenever I want."

An image appeared in my mind, of Lacey, clad in tight leather chaps and a leather halter top, climbing on the back of my bike and wrapping her arms around my waist.

Then taking off, the roar of my pipes, the wind in my face...and Lacey clinging to me.

"I understand. Really, I do."

"You don't. You sit here in your tight-ass office wearing your tight-ass suit, when you should be outdoors enjoying life."

"Mr. Wolfe, I—"

"Rock," I said. "Damn it. Call me Rock." My groin was tightening, and I couldn't stand it any longer.

I grabbed her and crushed my mouth to hers.

She kept her lips pinned shut, but I traced my tongue over the seam of them, nudging them open. "That's right, baby. Open for me." I swept my tongue into the warmth of her mouth.

She tasted minty fresh with a touch of vanilla. Delicious.

I glided my lips over hers as our tongues slid together.

I'd kissed a lot of women. Almost every weekend I took a new luscious treat to my bed.

But this kiss...

She pulled away and pushed at me.

I didn't move.

"Mr.—"

"Rock, damn it. I just had my tongue in your mouth. Call me Rock."

"Rock..." She swayed a little, steadying herself by placing her hand on the edge of her desk.

I couldn't help smiling.

"This... I'm not... This isn't...professional."

"It's not? That was a damned good kiss, baby. I'd say you could do it professionally."

Her cheeks went from rosy to crimson. Again, I smiled.

"You know what I mean."

"You're my father's lawyer. You're not mine. You and I don't have a professional relationship."

"It's not—"

I quieted her by placing two fingers over her pink, swollen lips. "You know what I'd like to do, Lacey Ward?"

She gulped.

"I'd like to lift up that blue skirt and bend you over that desk." I inched closer to her. "I bet you're already wet for me."

She squirmed, crossing her legs.

Yup. She was wet.

I inhaled. I could already smell her musky arousal. I inched forward again, until only a few centimeters separated us.

She backed up against her desk. "I don't think—"

"Don't think, baby. Now isn't the time for thinking. Where the hell would thinking get us? Just give in. Turn around." I lightly touched her arms, turning her around. Then I buried my nose in her neck and inhaled. "You smell like a fantasy."

"I'm not wearing anything." She let out a nervous chuckle. "Any perfume, I mean."

"I know. I smell *you*. I smell your arousal. You want me just as much as I want you." I grabbed the firm globes of her ass.

She let out a soft gasp.

I massaged her ass softly, pushing my hard cock into the small of her back. "You feel that? I'm hard for you, Lacey.

Rock hard. Tell me what you want me to do with that fucking hard cock."

"I want..." She moaned when I slid one hand up her side and then around in front to cup one firm breast.

"Yeah? What do you want, baby?"

"You. God. Fuck me. Fuck me hard."

All I needed. I slid her skirt up. Fuck. She was wearing a garter belt and stockings. I didn't know women wore those in an office anymore. And it was fucking hot.

And a thong. A pink lacy thong.

Lacey. Maybe she wasn't named after lingerie, but she was wearing it, lace and all. Her taut luscious body had been created for it.

"I'm going to rip this off of you and shove my hard cock into that hot pussy."

She groaned.

"Tell me you want it, baby. Tell me."

"God, yes. I want it."

With one yank, the pink thong was gone. I tossed it aside. Then I slid my fingers through her slick folds. God, so wet. I pulled my fingers out of her and ran them over my tongue. Mmm, sweet and tangy. If I weren't so fucking hard, I'd bend down and bury my face between those gorgeous ass cheeks and suck on that tasty pussy.

Next time. Not this time. This time would be fast and furious and delicious.

I unbuckled my belt and unzipped my jeans, releasing my erection. I slid it between her ass cheeks, teasing her.

"Please," she sighed. "I need you."

"Since you said please." I stopped for a few seconds to roll on a condom and then thrust into her.

She let out a low moan.

Yeah, that husky voice that had made me horny when she was reading the will. That's how I wanted to hear it, moaning as I fucked her.

"Feel good, baby? You like that?"

She inhaled sharply. "God, yes."

I pulled out and slid back in balls deep. Already my nuts were tightening, crushing to my body. This wouldn't take long.

But I wanted it to. Screw fast and furious. I wanted to fuck her long and slow and deep.

I pulled out and plunged in again. God, sweet suction. I wanted to touch her clit, rub it, make her come, but I couldn't in this position.

"Play with yourself, baby," I whispered into her ear. "Make it feel good." I grabbed her hand and led it around her front and under her skirt. "I'm not going to last long. You have such a tight cunt. I want to come inside you. Fill you up."

"I can't believe I'm doing this," she said on a sigh.

"Believe it, baby. Feel me. This is real. Feel me fucking you right here in your office."

Continue reading *Rebel* here!

A NOTE FROM HELEN

Dear Reader,

Thank you for reading *Opal*. If you want to find out about my current backlist and future releases, please visit my website, like my Facebook page, and join my mailing list. If you're a fan, please join my Facebook street team (Hardt & Soul) to help spread the word about my books. I regularly do awesome giveaways for my street team members.

If you enjoyed the story, please take the time to leave a review. I welcome all feedback.

I wish you all the best!

Helen

ACKNOWLEDGMENTS

Thank you so much to the following individuals who helped make this story shine: My editor (and son!), Eric McConnell, my cover artists, Kim Killion and Amanda Shepard, and my awesome beta readers, Karen Aguilera, Serena Drummond, Linda Pantlin Dunn, and Angela Tyler. You all rock!

ALSO BY HELEN HARDT

My Heart Still Beats

Bellamy Brothers
Savage Sin
Sweet Sin
Seductive Sin

Follow Me Series
Follow Me Darkly
Follow Me Under
Follow Me Always
Darkly
Under

Black Rose Series
Blush
Bloom
Blossom

Also by Helen Hardt

Wolfes of Manhattan
Rebel
Recluse
Runaway
Rake
Reckoning
Escape
Moonstone
Raven
Garnet
Buck
Opal
Phoenix
Amethyst

Sex and the Season
Lily and the Duke
Rose in Bloom
Lady Alexandra's Lover
Sophie's Voice
The Perils of Patricia

Steel Brothers Saga
Craving
Obsession
Possession
Melt
Burn
Surrender
Shattered
Twisted
Unraveled

ABOUT THE AUTHOR

#1 *New York Times*, #1 *USA Today*, and #1 *Wall Street Journal* bestselling author Helen Hardt's passion for the written word began with the books her mother read to her at bedtime. She wrote her first story at age six and hasn't stopped since. In addition to being an award-winning author of romantic fiction, she's a mother, an attorney, a black belt in Taekwondo, a grammar geek, an appreciator of fine red wine, and a lover of Ben and Jerry's ice cream. She writes from her home in Colorado, where she lives with her family. Helen loves to hear from readers.

Please sign up for her newsletter here:
http://www.helenhardt.com/signup
Visit her here:
http://www.helenhardt.com